Abigail

Adams

Girl of Colonial Days

Illustrated by James Ponter

Abigail Adams

Girl of Colonial Days

By Jean Brown Wagoner

Aladdin Paperbacks

Aladdin Paperbacks
An imprint of Simon & Schuster
Children's Publishing Division
1230 Avenue of the Americas
New York, NY 10020
Copyright © 1949, 1962 by the Bobbs-Merrill Company, Inc.
First Aladdin Paperbacks edition, 1992

Printed in the United States of America
10

Library of Congress Cataloging-in-Publication Data
Wagoner, Jean Brown, date.
    Abigail Adams : girl of colonial days / by Jean Brown Wagoner;
[illustrated by James Ponter]—1st Aladdin Books ed.
        p.   cm. — (Childhood of Famous Americans)
    Summary: A biography focusing on the early years of the parson's
daughter who became the wife of our second president.
    ISBN 0-689-71657-5
    1. Adams, Abigail, 1744-1818—Juvenile literature.   2. Adams, John,
1735-1826—Juvenile literature.   3. Presidents—United States—
Wives—Biography—Juvenile literature.   [1. Adams, Abigail, 1744-
1818—Childhood and youth.   2. First ladies.]   I. Title.   II. Series.
E322.1.A38W34   1992
973.4'4'092—dc20
[B]   92-345

*To the boys and girls of the Summer
Reading Club of the Irvington branch
of the Indianapolis Public Library*

Illustrations

Full pages

Numerous smaller illustrations

Contents

★ ★ Abigail Adams

Girl of Colonial Days

A Stormy Beginning

IT WAS a bad night. The snow fell thick and fast. A driving wind whipped it across the countryside and plastered it against anything that stood in its way.

The little town of Weymouth, Massachusetts, had more than its share of the storm. The houses were a solid white. No road or pathway showed. Even the river was covered. Only the steeple of the meetinghouse on top of the hill rose up bare and dark against the sky.

There was no sign of life anywhere in the village except at the Reverend Smith's house. Lights shone from every window there.

People were moving about. Suddenly a door was opened. An Indian darted out into the night. He flew over the snowy ground as swiftly as a deer. The runner was sure-footed and knew every inch of the way. The drifts and hidden ditches didn't stop him. In no time at all he was out of sight of the neighboring houses, the silent blacksmith shop, and the meetinghouse. Soon he was well on his way toward Boston.

At the Reverend Smith's house, the women watched the Indian when he sped away in the darkness. Then they turned back to the kitchen to prepare a feast. The smell of good things cooking filled the house.

In an upstairs room Mrs. Smith looked anxiously at the baby she held in her arms. "The baby is tiny," she said to her husband, "but don't you think she's a little better? I'm sure she seems stronger and is breathing more easily than she did at first."

The Reverend Smith thought the baby wasn't any worse, but he didn't know. The grandmother, Mrs. John Quincy, didn't like to say what she thought. She just shook her head doubtfully at the baby's Aunt Elizabeth, who took the word downstairs to the other aunts, Mary and Anna.

"The little thing is about the same, I guess," she said. "It's just as well that the Indian runner went after the baby's Grandfather Quincy. I doubt if she will live another day."

At dawn, Tom, the Reverend Smith's hired man, went out to the barn and hitched up the horse. He began to clear the road between the parsonage and the meetinghouse by dragging a heavy log over it.

As he passed the Burrells' house next to the Smiths', the maid, Dinah, came out. She called, "Why on earth are you doing that, Tom? Nobody's going to call at the preacher's today."

"Oh, yes, they will," said Tom. "Reverend Smith's going to baptize his baby daughter today. Her grandfather will be here."

"They won't take a baby out in weather like this, will they? She's only a week old."

"They have to," said Tom sadly. "She's very sickly and not lively to live. The mother wants her to have a name, so they're going ahead with the christening."

"So the baby's no better? That's too bad," Dinah said. "I'd better run tell Mrs. Burrell. She'll want to know."

Tom went on his way. At every house neighbors stopped him. "Why are you making a path today?" they wanted to know. In no time at all everyone in town had the word.

Within a few minutes Mrs. Burrell was at the Reverend Smith's door. She carried a covered bowl. The baby's grandmother, Mrs. Quincy, came to the door.

14

"I just heard about the baby," Mrs. Burrell explained. "I'm sorry she's no better. I brought over some medicine that I've always used for my children when they were sick. If you'll give a spoonful to the baby right away, I'm sure it will help her. Give her a spoonful every hour until she is better."

Mrs. Quincy thanked the neighbor and took the medicine upstairs to Mrs. Smith's room. "Mrs. Burrell brought this for the baby," she said. She lifted the lid off the bowl. "Whew!" she cried when she smelled it. "It must be spoiled. I'll throw it out."

"No, no," said Mrs. Smith. "If Mrs. Burrell used it, it must be all right. Her children are well and strong."

So Grandmother lifted the little baby out of the cradle and gave her a taste. The baby screamed and cried. Grandmother walked the floor with her until the child fell asleep.

Before she could put the baby down, Mrs. Pratt, another neighbor, was at the door. Mrs. Pratt brought a tonic that was good for colic. Before she left, Mrs. Whitman came.

Soon the grandmother and the three aunts were kept busy answering the door. Even little Mary, the baby's sister, ran to let people in. Everybody loved the Reverend Smith and Mrs. Smith. Everybody wanted to do something to help save the baby.

"I don't know where we're going to put all the medicine," Grandmother said. "I've given the baby more than is good for her."

"The sooner we have the christening the better," said Aunt Mary.

"I wanted to wait for the baby's Grandfather Quincy," said the mother. "I don't want to have the christening until he comes."

"He can never get through these drifts," said Mrs. Whitman. "You can't see the road."

"A snowstorm won't stop Colonel John Quincy," said the Reverend Smith. "He'll be here." Just as he finished speaking there were glad shouts outside. Grandfather Quincy was coming up the hill on horseback.

"Who are those people with him?" Mrs. Whitman asked.

"Why, it's the chief of the Ponkapoag Indians and the Indian runner, Robert, who went to bring him," said Grandmother Quincy in a pleased voice. "They've come to honor the granddaughter of their friend. We must dress the baby quickly and take her down. The chief will want to see her."

The aunts began to get together things the baby was to wear. There were stacks of long petticoats trimmed with lace and embroidery. There was a dress of finest cambric that Mother had worn when she was christened. Aunt Anna brought a hood she had made for her niece.

17

Aunt Elizabeth had a silk jacket she had embroidered, and Aunt Mary had woven a blanket of soft white wool.

Everyone crowded around to see the baby when they carried her downstairs. Even Phoebe, the cook, left the kitchen, and the extra help came, too, to look.

"She's a little angel," Phoebe said, wiping the tears from her eyes.

"Let me see," said Mary who was two years old. "Let me see the baby."

Aunt Mary lifted up the little girl. "There's your baby sister," she said.

"May I play with her?" asked Mary.

"You'll have to wait till she's older," Aunt Mary answered.

The other aunts looked sad. "The poor baby will never live to run and play," they thought.

"What's everyone so glum about?" said a hearty voice. It was Grandfather Quincy.

"We're so worried about our grandchild," whispered Grandmother. "We don't think she'll live. She's so small and thin."

"Let me see her. Where is she?" asked Grandfather. "Let me see my granddaughter."

Grandmother brought the baby to him.

"I thought you said she was thin," Grandfather said cheerfully. "This baby's fat." No wonder he thought so. She had so many clothes on she looked like a little fat pillow. "I've seen babies much smaller than this who grew up to be fine, strong people. She'll be all right. We'll be proud of her someday," he boasted. "What do you think, Chief Mummentaug?"

Grandmother laid the baby in the chief's arms. The chief smiled in a very friendly, kindly way. "She's little," he said, "but she'll live to be a great lady like her grandmother." He handed the baby back to Mrs. Quincy. "Here is a little gift the Indian women made for her."

19

He gave Mrs. Quincy a beautiful doeskin robe. The Reverend Smith thanked the chief. The aunts and the grandmother thanked him, too.

"Now, we really must go," Grandmother said. "It's getting colder every minute, Tom says."

When they went outside they agreed Tom was right. The icy wind took their breath away. It tugged at the women's shawls and flapped the men's coattails.

The Reverend Smith led the way to make a path through the drifts. Grandmother came next, with the baby in her arms. The other members of the family came after them in single file. Neighbors came out and joined them. Most of the village went to the meetinghouse.

While they were outside, Grandmother didn't dare lift the robe to look at the baby. The minute they were inside the building she peeked under the covers. She sighed with relief. The baby was sound asleep.

When the Reverend Smith went to baptize his tiny little girl, he found the water frozen in the font. "I had no idea it would freeze inside here, so soon," he said.

There wasn't any heat in the meetinghouse. There never was. The grownups were used to it, but he was afraid for the baby and wanted to baptize her quickly. He struck the ice with his knuckles, but it wouldn't break. He looked about for something heavy. The handle of a hunting knife would be just the thing. But of course none of the men carried knives in their good clothes.

The old chief saw what the trouble was. He handed the Reverend Smith his tomahawk. With this, he broke the ice easily and went on with the ceremony. Grandmother named the baby "Abigail" for the Reverend Smith's mother.

No one stayed long after the baptizing. Grandmother wanted to get the baby to a warm place.

The others were thinking of the Smiths' warm house and the wonderful food they had smelled in the kitchen. There was always a feast after baptizing, and they were hungry after their walk in the snow and the cold wind.

The aunts and Phoebe had been cooking for days to have enough food ready. There were roasted turkeys and chickens and geese, and beef and ham on the kitchen tables. The pantry shelves were loaded with pies and custards and puddings and cakes. The cellar steps were lined with preserves and pickles and relishes. And in the big brick oven next to the open fireplace, pans of corn bread were browning.

When the little group reached the house everything was ready, and all of it looked delicious. But no one touched the food until the father had offered a prayer. Then he carefully wrote in the church record, "I baptized my daughter Abigail today, November 18, 1744."

Little Mary leaned against her father's knee and watched him write. "What are you saying there?" she asked.

"I'm writing your sister's name in the record."

"What is her name?" asked Mary.

"It's Abigail," answered Father.

"That's a nice name. I like it," Mary said. She ran over to tell her aunts what it was.

"What did you say it was?" they asked.

"Nabby," said Mary.

"You made a mistake," Aunt Elizabeth said. "It's Abigail."

"That's what I said—'Nabby,'" repeated Mary. That was as close as she could get to "Abigail." It wasn't long before everyone called the baby "Nabby."

For days and weeks the neighbors stopped in to ask how Nabby was. Each time they went away shaking their heads. "She won't be here the next time we come," they'd say. But she was!

Finally they all knew that she was going to live. Then everyone was happy. Each of the good neighbor women thought to herself, "It was the fine medicine *I* brought that saved her. If it hadn't been for me, there wouldn't be any little Abigail Smith."

Grandfather bragged, "I told you all along she was going to be all right."

Abigail's Wish

"COME AWAY from the window, Nabby," said
Mrs. Smith one morning to six-year-old Abigail.
"It's chilly over there. You might catch cold
and get sick again."

Abigail had been watching Mary go off to
school. It was a bright spring day and it didn't
seem chilly to her, but she came over to the fireplace at once. She'd been sick, and this was her
first day downstairs in a long time. She didn't
want to have to go to bed again.

There wasn't a sound in the room for a while.
Mother was mending. Abigail sat and looked at
the fire without saying a word.

This was the time of day when she usually had her reading lesson, and she liked to read. To-day, though, she didn't even look at her primer.

It wasn't like her to be quiet so long. Mother asked anxiously, "You aren't feeling worse, are you, Nabby? Don't you want to lie down?"

"No," said Abigail, "I was just thinking. It isn't any fun being sick. I'm six years old, and I can't go any place or do anything. Mary has lots of good times. She goes to school, and plays with her friends and slides downhill in the winter. Will gets to ride with Father all over town, and he's only four." Will was her little brother. "Even the baby goes more than I do. You take her with you to see Grandmother and the aunts."

"Nabby, as soon as you get stronger, you may do the things your brothers and sisters do," said her mother patiently.

"All I can do is sit at home and take smelly old medicine," Abigail complained.

She was sorry the minute she said that. Mother glanced at the clock. "Dear me," she said, "it's way past time for your tonic. Run and take a dose right away. It's on the bottom shelf in the pantry. Don't go through the study, remember. Father is teaching a class."

"Who's there?" Abigail asked. She knew very well that it was John Adams and Samuel Adams and Josiah Quincy. She was only trying to put off taking the medicine.

"Don't dillydally, Nabby," said Mother.

Abigail took as long as she dared to get to the pantry. All the way she said to herself, "I wish the house would fall down or something would happen right now. But it won't. It never does, for me." She pushed the pantry door open.

"Nabby!" someone screamed. Abigail jumped back so quickly she bumped her head against the chimney corner. It was Phoebe, the old cook, who had shouted.

"Don't you dare go into the pantry," Phoebe scolded. "Can't you see the floor has just been painted? Why don't you look sometimes?"

"I didn't notice," said Abigail.

"Tom's had to do it over twice already. Yesterday the dog ran in on it, so I had Tom paint it again this morning. I'll take a stick to anyone who sets a foot in it before it's dry. Do you understand that?"

"Yes'm," said Nabby happily. She ran to tell Mother she couldn't take her tonic. She couldn't get into the pantry.

"Phoebe probably took the medicine out before the floor was painted," Mother said. "Go ask her if she didn't."

Abigail went back slowly. Sure enough, Phoebe had set the nasty stuff in the warming oven. She brought it out. At that moment the kitchen door flew open and Tom came in with an armload of wood.

Behind Tom came Will, and behind Will came
the dog, Rover. Rover darted in before anyone
could stop him. He saw Abigail and began to
bark and and run around her in circles.

Will shouted with laughter. "Good old Rover, he knows you've been sick. He's glad to see you. Look at him go!"

Rover certainly did go. He tore through the house and back again. He jumped clear over Abigail's head and bumped into Phoebe, and knocked the medicine bowl out of her hands. It crashed on the hearth.

Phoebe snatched up the broom and ran after the pup. Rover saw that the fun was over. He looked for a place to hide, and darted into the pantry under a shelf.

"Now see what's happened," Phoebe wailed. "Look at my nice new floor!" She shook her broom at Rover. "Git!" she cried. "Get out!"

But Rover wouldn't. Instead he crawled to the farthest corner and lay there panting.

"Get that dog out of there," she cried.

Will went to the door and coaxed. "Here, Rover! Here, Rover!"

Rover thumped his tail, but wouldn't come.

Tom went to the door and snapped his fingers. "Come on, Rover, come on!"

Rover laid his head between his paws and pretended not to hear.

Abigail went to the door. "Here, Rover! Here, Rover!" she called cheerily.

Rover wagged all over, but didn't come.

"He's afraid," said Abigail. "Maybe if Phoebe would put the broom down and stand back of the door he'd come."

Phoebe thought that a good idea. "Tom," she ordered, "you stand at the door to the front part of the house. Don't let that dog get past you now. He'll track up everything. Will, hold the back door open. I'll be here ready to shoo him out. All right now, Miss Nabby, call him again."

"Here, Rover! Here, puppy!" Abigail called.

This time the dog come running and jumped up on her. She ran to the door and let him out.

"Of all the nuisances that ever were, that dog's the worst," said Phoebe. "I'm going to tell Mrs. Smith that either he goes or I go."

Will began to cry at that.

"Look at this kitchen," complained Phoebe. "I'll never get that medicine stain out of the floor. It'll go right through the wood."

Abigail had forgotten about her tonic. She was glad it was on the floor and not inside her.

Then Phoebe saw Abigail's dress. It was smeared with paint. "Look at your dress! When your mother sees it she'll send the dog away."

Will began to cry harder than ever.

"What is the matter?" asked Mrs. Smith. She had come to the kitchen to see why Will was crying. "You'll wake the baby and disturb your father and his students. They can't think with so much noise going on." Then she, too, saw Abigail's dress. "Goodness, Nabby, what happened? Did you fall in the paint bucket?"

"The dog jumped on her, that's what happened," said Phoebe. "He tracked the floor again, too. Just look at that floor!"

"Rover didn't know any better," Abigail said anxiously. "You won't send him away, will you? We'll teach him to behave."

"We'll have to do something with him," said her mother, "at least until the paint's dry. We don't seem to be able to keep him out of the house, and he does too much damage."

"Let's send him to Grandmother Quincy's," Abigail suggested. "She'll take care of him."

"Who could take him there? Tom's busy planting the garden. Your father's busy with his class today, and he is too busy, anyway."

"Why can't Tom hitch up the horse? You drive, and we'll all go. I haven't seen Grandmother since I was sick." Abigail and Will thought this was a very good idea. They always liked to go to Grandmother Quincy's.

Mother shook her head. "The roads are too soft since the spring rains began. The wheels would sink in mud up to the hub. It will be several weeks before the ground is hard enough for driving. We would get stuck in the mud before we'd gone a mile, and we'd probably tear a wheel from the carriage trying to get out!"

"What will you do with him, then? You won't kill him, will you?" Abigail asked, terribly upset. Will began to cry again.

"No, of course I won't kill him," Mother said. "Phoebe, tell Tom to catch Rover and tie him in the barn. You run along upstairs, Nabby, and change your dress."

Abigail went up and took off the dress. She was about to take it back downstairs to Phoebe, when she had an idea. "I know how I can take the paint out, and it won't be any trouble at all. I'll do it and surprise Mother and Phoebe. I wonder why they didn't think of it."

Quick as a flash she popped into Mother's room and took the scissors from her workbox. Very carefully she cut all around the paint spots. She had watched Mother cut out patterns that way. It was as easy as cutting cookies. The spots lifted right out.

She put the dress back on and started downstairs, feeling quite happy. She took a last look at herself. Oh, dear! Something was wrong! There were holes where the spots had been, and they looked bad. Her petticoat showed through. She would have to do something about them.

Once more she went to Mother's workbox. This time she used a needle and thread. She sewed around the holes, then pulled the thread tight. The holes were gone!

"Nabby, what's taking you so long?" Mother called from the foot of the stairs. "If we don't get that paint out right away, it will never come out. We're waiting for the dress."

"You won't have to take it out," Abigail cried happily. "I've already done it, all by myself, too. Look!" She ran into the kitchen and turned around, showing the dress proudly.

Mother couldn't say a word at first. Phoebe clucked her tongue. "Why, Nabby, what are all those gathered places?"

Abigail looked down. The dress hung every which way. Wherever there had been a hole the goods was pulled into a knot. Abigail hadn't noticed it before.

"What on earth were you trying to do?" Mother asked when she had looked at it closely. "Why did you cut your dress?"

"I thought I was helping you." The longer Abigail looked at her dress, the worse she felt. She began to cry. "Don't you think we can fill the holes up again? Can't we sew the spots back-in? Show me how, Mother, and I'll sew them in myself. You won't have to do it."

Mother shook her head. "The dress is ruined. It is good only for rags now. I'll have to punish you for this, Nabby. I know you didn't mean to be naughty, but you'll have to learn to think before you do things. It will take all of us days and days to spin enough yarn for another dress. If you had thought one minute, it would have saved us all a lot of time."

Abigail had to go to bed for the rest of the day. That night she said to herself, "I was wishing something would happen today, and it did. But it was the wrong kind of thing. I'm going to be more careful about my wishes after this."

Gunpowder in the Meetinghouse

It was Saturday afternoon. Father and the children were on their way to the meetinghouse. As they passed the Burrell's house Abigail said, "I'd better run in and ask Mrs. Burrell if she has any letters she wants posted."

"It's too late to catch the post today," Father said. "The postman must have gone through Weymouth some time ago."

"Oh, no, Father. Mr. Turner's horse went lame, and he had to get another at Roxbury, so he's late. People can still send letters."

Mr. Turner was the postrider. He brought the mail from Boston twice a week.

He always stopped a few minutes at the blacksmith shop in Weymouth. As soon as people saw his horses tied outside, they took him the letters they wanted to send and picked up any mail he had for them.

"How do you know about Mr. Turner's horse?" Father asked.

"Toby told me a while ago when he brought in the eggs," said Nabby.

Toby was the blacksmith's son. He helped Tom with the chores on Saturdays.

"Have you any letters to send, Mrs. Burrell?" Abigail called.

"Why, Nabby, I'm glad to see you're well again! Yes, I have a letter. I thought I had missed Mr. Turner. It's late, and I didn't see his horse."

Abigail told her about the lame horse. They would have talked for a long time, but Mary called, "Nabby, the others have gone on."

Abigail ran, and she and Mary soon caught up. As they passed Mrs. Bicknell's, Mary said, "Don't stop here, Nabby. She talks too long."

"She may be watching for me," said Abigail. "I'll have to stop, but I'll hurry."

Mrs. Bicknell was waiting at the door when Abigail ran up the walk. "It's good to see you out again, Nabby. I was hoping you'd stop." She handed the little girl a letter. "You're the only one who remembers how hard it is for me to climb the hill from the blacksmith shop. Why is Mr. Turner so late today?"

Abigail told her about the lame horse, and then skipped to catch up with the others.

"Now please don't stop at Mrs. Trudy's," begged Mary. "She's a mean old gossip. I wouldn't do anything for her."

But when they came to her place, Abigail went inside, although she would have been glad to skip this one house.

Mrs. Trudy didn't have any letters, but she kept Abigail and asked a lot of questions. Why was the Reverend Smith going to the meeting-house at this time of day? What were the names on Mrs. Burrell's and Mrs. Bicknell's letters? Why was Abigail wearing her second-best dress? "Be sure to stop in on your way home and tell me who got letters today," she called after Abigail. "Don't forget, now."

Father and Will were at the foot of the hill by that time. The girls had little hopes of catching up to them.

"I don't think I like Mrs. Trudy," said Abigail. She told Mary about all the questions while they hurried along.

"You won't stop at Mrs. Pratt's, will you?" asked Mary. "She lives too far up on the hill."

But Mrs. Pratt was out on her doorstep waving her shawl to catch their attention. "Pretend you don't see her," said Mary.

"I can't," said Abigail. "Look! She has a package she wants to send. It's probably for her son Billy, who is in the army at Fort Henry."

"Then I'll go see her with you," said Mary. They climbed the hill to Mrs. Pratt's house.

"You're so kind to come way up here," said Mrs. Pratt. "I was too tired to get down to the smithy this afternoon, and Billy needs this shirt so badly. It's freezing cold up north, and he's sick. I'm so worried about him."

Abigail said she would tell Mr. Turner about Billy. He would send the shirt on by the first messenger. Mr. Turner would do all he could to see that Billy got the shirt right away.

"Now we'll have to run," said Mary, "but I'm glad we stopped. You were right, Abigail. We musn't miss any of the places."

At home Mother and Phoebe were looking out the window, watching the two girls as they went from house to house for the letters.

"Just look at that little Nabby," Phoebe was saying. "She's the friendliest little girl in the whole country—always looking out for other people. There isn't another child in town who's as thoughtful as she is."

"I'm glad she's friendly," said Mother, "but I was just noticing how undignified she is. She runs and skips and jumps like a boy. That won't do. She's too old to run like that. I've been so anxious to keep her well I hadn't noticed her manners. I'm afraid people will talk. I must do something about it right away."

Mother needn't have worried. All the way to the blacksmith shop people waved and called to Abigail, "It's good to see you well again! The world is bright when you're around."

There was only one person who frowned. That was Mrs. Trudy. "Tch, tch, tch," she said, "what a tomboy Abigail is! I should think her mother would teach her how to behave."

Mary and Abigail caught up with Father and Will as they reached the meetinghouse. The sexton who looked after the building was just leaving. Father called out, "Wait a minute, Sam. I want to look at the garret." Father had to shout because Sam was hard of hearing.

"I was just up there," said Sam. "Everything's all right. You don't have to worry. I check up there every day."

"I'd better take a look, anyway," Father said. He went inside and up the stairs to the balcony. He came to the door that led to the garret. He felt along the molding until he found a key. "I'll be right back down," he told the children. He unlocked the door and went up.

Abigail started to follow him. "No, no," Sam called. "You mustn't go up. Children aren't allowed up there."

"Why not?" she asked. "I've often been up in the garret, and so have the other children."

45

"The town's supply of gunpowder is in the garret," Sam said. "Three barrels full, enough to blow us all to the next world. It's no place for children. We keep it locked now."

"What's Father doing up there?" Mary asked anxiously. "The gunpowder might blow up while he's in the garret."

"He's the preacher, and feels responsible for the whole town. He wants to be sure the gunpowder's dry. Rifles are stacked up there, too. He'll see that they're ready to use, in case we need them. We might want them in a hurry."

"Why do they keep the gunpowder in the meetinghouse?" Abigail asked Father, when he came down.

"That's the safest place," he said. "It's dry, and there aren't any fireplaces or chimneys in the building. No sparks can fly out and set it on fire. The only danger is that lightning might strike the steeple and set the powder off."

46

Abigail swallowed. "What if a storm came up while we were all in church?"

"I'd tell everyone to run outside and wait till the storm was over," Father said. "That happened once while I was preaching."

"I wish it would happen when I'm there," Will said. Father's sermons seemed awfully long to him. He found it very hard to sit still.

"I wish we didn't have to keep the gunpowder at all!" Abigail said.

"Every town has to have it handy," Father said. "Towns farther north need it to fight the French and the Indians. We don't, because your Grandfather Quincy made friends with the Indians that lived in this part of the country.

"When I was a boy, French and Spanish pirates landed boats on our coast and came into the small towns for supplies. They kidnapped boys and men and made slaves of them."

"Pirates don't come any more, do they?"

"The English gunboats in Boston bay have scared them away from these shores now. We're really safe, but we want gunpowder in case anything happens to the English Navy."

By this time Father and the children were out of the meetinghouse, going down the hill. "There's Mr. Turner's horse!" cried Abigail. "He did get here!"

"We'll stop and pick up the mail," Father said. At the blacksmith shop he went in to talk to Mr. Turner and learn the news from Boston and towns along the way. The children saw Toby and some of the neighbor boys outside. They went to see what the boys were doing.

Toby and Benjie Bicknell were making bullets. Lars White and Jack Whitman and Isaac Webb were cleaning their fathers' rifles.

"We're going to have a shooting contest in a minute," they said. "You children can watch us if you keep out of the way."

These boys were older than the Smith children. They knew all about guns.

"We can stay till Father is ready," said Mary.

The boys set up a target and began to shoot. Isaac was a fine shot. So was Jack, but Benjie didn't hit near the mark.

"I could do better than that," said Will. "I could hit the target."

"You could not," said Benjie. "You're too little. You can't even hold a rifle steady, much less shoot it. Just let me see you do it." He laid his gun at Will's feet.

Will tried to lift it to his shoulder. His face grew red as a beet. His eyes were popping but he couldn't manage it.

"Give up, Will," said Toby. "You're too little to handle a gun. When you're older, you'll be able to hit the target all right."

Toby didn't mean to hurt Will's feelings, but Will's cheeks burned.

"Even if you could hold the rifle, we couldn't let you fire it," Toby said, "because we've used up all our powder."

"I wish we could get some more," said Lars. "We won't ever be good marksmen if we can't practice shooting more."

"I know where there's plenty of powder," said Will. He wanted to make the boys notice him.

"So do we," jeered Benjie. "There's more than enough on the warships at Boston." The boys thought that was awfully funny. They howled and laughed at Benjie's joke.

"This is a lot closer," Will said loudly. "It's kept right up there in the meetinghouse garret."

"Everybody knows that," hooted Isaac. "But we can't get any of it, and neither can you. No one knows where Sam keeps the key."

"I know where it is," Will bragged. He remembered seeing Father reach up over the doorway to get the key and later to put it back.

The boys were quiet at this. "Do you really know, Will?" asked Toby finally.

Will nodded. Mary and Abigail wished he would keep quiet. They knew he shouldn't tell.

"I'm going to Father," said Mary. She went inside, but Abigail stayed.

"Tell us, and we'll let you shoot," said Isaac.

"I'll hold my gun steady and let you fire as often as you like," promised Benjie.

"We'll make some fizzcrackers and fire them off down at the riverbank," Toby promised. "I'll make you some, too, and you can go with us to set them off. Would you like that?"

This was too much for Will. He couldn't get the words out fast enough. "The key's up over the doorway to the garret."

"If we aren't dumb!" said Benjie. "Why didn't we think of looking there!"

"Let's go get the powder right now," cried Jack. "Who's game to go?"

"We can't go up there in daylight," Toby said. "Everybody in town would see us. We'll have to wait till everyone's gone to bed. We'll go together—all except Will. He's too young."

"Let's do it tonight," Isaac said.

Abigail had kept still as long as she could. "You'd better not," she said. "It would be wrong to take the powder. That's to fight the French and Indians with."

The boys grinned. "Listen to Nabby," Jack said. "The French and Indians don't come around here. Have you ever seen any?"

"Anyhow, we're only going to take a little," said Benjie. "No one will miss it."

"What if you're caught?" Abigail asked.

"We're not going to get caught," Toby said. "We'll be as still as ghosts."

"Ghosts aren't still," Abigail argued. "Phoebe says they make a lot of noise. They go 'OOooooo-OOOoooOOO!' "

"Oh, they don't either. There aren't any ghosts, so how could they make a noise?" said Toby. But he turned a little pale. He wished Abigail hadn't said that. "You spoil everything," he said sourly. "Now don't you go tell anyone on us. Don't be a tattletale."

"You know I won't tell," said Abigail. "But I wish you wouldn't go up there." She wanted to beg the boys not to, but Father came out of the shop just then, so she had to leave.

Abigail and the Ghosts

"NABBY, you're not eating a thing," Mother said at the supper table that evening. "I do hope you're not going to be sick. You'd better take some tonic. You really look peaked."

Abigail knew what was the matter. All the tonic in the world couldn't help her. She was worried about the gunpowder. One minute she thought, "What if lightning strikes the steeple while boys are up there? They'll be killed, and it will be my fault for not stopping them."

Another minute she thought, "If they take gunpowder this time, they'll take it whenever they want it, and more each time."

She tried to eat, but the food almost choked her. "When the Indians come, there won't be any powder left to fight with," she thought. "We'll all be killed. I just have to do something, and I'll have to do it soon."

But she couldn't think of a thing to do.

She went to bed as soon as supper was over. "You'd better not get up in the morning," said Mother. "I'll let Mary sleep in the corner room, so she won't waken you."

Abigail heard everyone come upstairs to bed. Phoebe was the last of all. She creaked up to her room in the attic.

Abigail sat by the window and stared into the dark. She wondered what time it was. The house was still. Downstairs, Rover gave a loud yawn and lay down by the fireplace.

Rover was a good watchdog. He didn't make any noise at night, unless a wolf or a fox got into the barn lot. Then he would make a great racket.

"I wish Rover was at the meetinghouse. He'd keep the boys away. He'd make such a fuss even old Sam would wake up and come to find out what the trouble was."

Abigail thought a minute. "If I could get Rover into the meetinghouse, the boys wouldn't have a chance to get any of the powder."

She wished Will were older, so she could have him take the dog. She didn't think Mary would go, nor let her little sister go.

"I guess I'll have to take him myself," she said. She dressed and wrapped herself in a long shawl, and crept downstairs. Rover got up from the fireplace and came over to the window. He licked her hand.

"Come on, Rover," she whispered. She opened the door. They slipped through without making a sound. Down the hill they ran. "I hope we're in time," she panted as they climbed the hill to the meetinghouse.

The moon came out and shone brightly over the countryside. Abigail could see everywhere, but she kept her eyes glued to the ground. The graveyard lay close by.

"Phoebe says that ghosts come out and sit on the tombstones at night," she whispered to Rover. "Father says there aren't any ghosts. I just won't look that way," she decided. She hurried to open the meetinghouse door.

"Come in, Rover," she called softly.

But the dog wouldn't come. He had been trained to stay outside. She had to pull him in by the scruff of his neck.

"Now, Rover," she said, "You stay here. Bark loud when the boys come. Go Grruff!"

Rover looked at her sadly.

"Now stay!" she ordered. "Stay still." She patted him and went out. But she was barely outside when Rover gave a long, low howl. She went back to him on the run.

"Don't make any noise yet!" she whispered. "Wait until the boys come!"

Rover jumped up and licked her face. He wagged his tail as if to say, "Come on, let's go home now. I don't like this game."

"Down, Rover, down!" said Abigail, wiping her face. "You have to save the gunpowder. You have to stay here."

She went away again, but had to come right back. She tried it again and again. Rover howled and whined. She tried to explain to him. "If the boys come and find me here, they won't be afraid at all. You've got to growl and bark before they see us. You've got to save the gunpowder."

Rover didn't understand in the least. He was very unhappy about being in there at all.

"I might as well take you back home," she said at last, and started to the door. At that moment she thought she heard footsteps. Her heart jumped. Someone was coming!

The steps were quite near. There wasn't time to get away. "Come, Rover," she whispered. She pulled him up the balcony steps. She ran to the garret door and turned. The door opened. Father must have forgotten to lock it.

Quickly she pushed Rover through, closed the door, and sat down on the bottom step beside the dog. She was thoroughly frightened.

Outside, close against the wall, crouched Toby, Isaac, Lars, Jack, and Benjie. "Did you hear something?" whispered Isaac.

"Yes," Benjie whispered back. "Like something dragging across the floor."

"I heard something before that," said Jack. "First I thought it was a dog howling. Then it sounded more like a ghost." He shivered.

"Oh, there isn't any such thing," said Toby. He sounded braver than he felt. "Come on, we'll stick together. If it's a ghost it'll have to get all of us." He giggled nervously.

They crept to the door, holding onto one another. They felt a little easier when they were inside and nothing had grabbed them. They stood still a minute to get used to the darkness. They heard a scratching at the garret door.

61

Rover was scratching because he wanted to get out, but the boys didn't know that. They froze in their tracks.

"That sounds just like a hoof," whispered Lars hoarsely. "They say the devil has hoofs. I'm going home right now."

"No, you can't go yet," Toby whispered. "You're just imagining things. That was probably a limb brushing against the window. What's everybody so scared of? Come on, let's go up."

He led the way boldly. The others followed in a tight little group.

They were at the front of the balcony steps, when the scraping sound came again. Everyone stopped, but Toby said, "I never saw such a bunch of cowards. I'm going on by myself. We can't stay here all night."

He went up slowly, a step at a time. The others waited at the bottom. They stared up into the darkness. Toby got to the top step.

Suddenly there came a low moan. The boys all stopped breathing. Then they heard a loud "OOOooooo OOOooooO!" The sound echoed until it seemed to be all around them.

Toby took a flying leap down the stairs. He landed on top of the boys below. With another leap he was on his way outside. Benjie, Lars, Isaac, and Jack were so close behind him that his coattails flapped in their faces. Not one of them turned his head, or slowed down till he was in his own house, in his own bed, with the covers pulled over his head.

Back at the meetinghouse, Abigail patted Rover on the head. "We can go home now," she said. "You're a good dog. Your howling scared them away. The powder is safe."

The little girl and the dog left the meetinghouse and ran home. They slipped back into the house, and no one heard them. Rover dropped by the fireplace, and Abigail went to bed.

Fire!

IT WAS a clear night many weeks later. Abigail was sure she hadn't fallen asleep, but all at once she felt the sun shining in her face. She sat up and rubbed her eyes, and looked out.

"Why, that's not the sun!" she cried. "It's a fire! The meetinghouse is on fire!" She jumped out of bed and ran to her father's room, calling out, "Father, Father, the meetinghouse is on fire! Hurry, Father!"

Father began throwing on his clothes and shouting out the upstairs windows to Tom and the neighbors, "Fire! Fire! The meetinghouse is on fire! Get everybody up!"

Abigail ran to the attic and wakened Phoebe. Mary pulled Will out of bed and hustled him downstairs. Mother carried the baby down. People were pouring out of their houses and running toward the meetinghouse.

"Stay back! Stay back!" cried Father in a voice like thunder. "The gunpowder will explode any moment. Don't let anyone go near." He set up guards all around the hill. "Get out the ladders," he ordered, "and be ready to put out any new fire that may start."

The gunpowder! Abigail had forgotten about it. Now she remembered what Sam had said. She was afraid. She ran to her mother. "I wish Father had stayed here to take care of us," she whimpered. "I wish he was here now."

"Father has the whole village to look after," said Mother. "We can take care of ourselves, can't we?" Mother didn't seem to be frightened at all. She talked quietly with the neighbors.

Abigail had been watching the fire for only a minute or two when there was a thundering roar. The gunpowder had exploded.

The meetinghouse roof blew up to the sky and fell in a million blazing pieces. The fire was so bright that it seemed brighter than the sun to Abigail. She could see everywhere. The people all over the hillside, the trees, the houses, the barns—all stood out as clear as day. She saw the red light on the patches of snow that remained along the brook in front of the house. She could even see the buds swelling on the lilac bush beside the front door.

The meetinghouse burned fast after the explosion. There was nothing left of it in a few hours. The men kept watch all night, though, to be sure that nothing else caught fire from the sparks.

Mother and the neighbor women made coffee and had kettles of soup for the watchers. There was nothing else they could do.

Unfair to Girls

ABIGAIL fairly gulped down her breakfast the next morning. She could hardly wait to get over to the hilltop where the meetinghouse had been. It was crowded with people. All the roads were jammed, too. She had never seen so many wagons and carts and carriages. There were a few fine big coaches, too. The river was filled with boats and canoes and rafts. All were loaded with sightseers.

"I guess there never was a fire as big as the one we had last night," she said. "It looks as if everyone in the world had heard the gunpowder go off, and come to see what happened."

She slid from her place at the table and went for her wrap. As she started to put it on, her mother spoke.

"Where are you going, Nabby?"

"I'm going to the meetinghouse to find out how the fire started and whether the ashes are still hot," she said. "I want to see the people who came in the coaches, too."

"Father has already gone. He'll tell you about it when he comes back," Mother said. "You mustn't go. You must learn to be a lady. Little girls don't belong in crowds like that. It's not considered nice."

Abigail thought she hadn't heard right. Not go to see everything? Miss all the excitement? Why, what could be the matter with Mother?

"I mean it," said Mother. "You're not to go. You're getting too big to run everywhere in town. Girls and ladies aren't supposed to be seen in public places."

"How do girls find out anything if they can't go where things are happening?" cried Abigail.

"Father will tell you everything you need to know," said Mother.

"He might forget some of it," said Abigail, "and you don't like for me to ask questions."

"That's right," said Mother. "There's still another thing you must remember. Ladies don't talk when the men are around. You're not a little girl any more. You'll soon be a young lady, and you must learn to act like one."

Mother saw Father coming up the hill toward the house. The church deacons were with him. "Remember now, Nabby," she said, "no questions. You don't want to be like Mrs. Trudy."

Abigail went up to her room and shut the door. "It's no fair being a girl," she said. She didn't go down when Father came. Usually she met him at the door, and told him all the news of the household.

"Where's Abigail?" he asked when he came in. He missed her cheerful talk. "She isn't sick, is she? She's seemed stronger lately."

Abigail didn't answer. After a while she said to herself, "I'm being silly. I won't ever find out about the fire if I stay up here."

She took her knitting, and went down to the parlor. She pulled her three-legged stool into a far corner, where she wouldn't be noticed. She listened for all she was worth.

Deacon White was talking. "Some people say the explosion was heard beyond Boston."

"They saw the light from it for twenty miles, or more," said another.

"Everyone is asking how the fire started," said Deacon Webb. "No one seems to have any real clue. I asked everywhere."

All the other deacons said the same thing. No one had heard or seen anything unusual around the meetinghouse.

Toby and his friends didn't know any more about it than anyone else. "It's a good thing the ghosts scared us away that night," he said. "We might have been blamed for the fire."

"We might have been blown up."

"I'm glad we learned our lesson and never went there again."

Abigail was glad, too.

Mice in the Attic

"MRS. SMITH! There are more folks coming up the hill to see where the fire was," Phoebe called one evening. "Where are we going to put them?"

It was suppertime. A wagonload of people had just pulled into the Smiths' lane.

Mother ran to the window. "We'll have to make room for them some way. They have little children with them. It's too late for them to go farther. The road through the woods is hard to follow after dark."

Several days had passed since the fire, but people were still coming to see where it had been. Whole families came. The womenfolk always spent the day at the Reverend Smith's. The men walked over the hill to look. Some stayed overnight. The parsonage was full to overflowing. This evening there were more visitors than usual. Mother was frantic. Where could she put these new people?

Abigail saw how worried her mother was. "Why don't you tell them there isn't enough room? We've had the house as full of people as it could be every day and night since the fire. Let them go somewhere else."

"I don't know where they'd go," her mother answered. "Mrs. Bicknell and Mrs. Burrell both have sickness in their families. Neither one of them could possibly take anyone in."

"How about Mrs. Trudy?" asked Abigail. "She has a big house. There are only three people in it—Mrs. Trudy and Mr. Trudy and their little girl, Silence."

"I don't like to ask her," Mother said. "She always says no to everything. Maybe this once, though, she might help. Will you go ask her for me? I don't think I could do it. She might be more inclined to say yes to you because you often do things for her."

Abigail went gladly. She was sure Mrs. Trudy would say yes to her, because she had run so many errands for her. The Trudys were at dinner. Mrs. Trudy said it was not polite of Abigail to call at such an hour. Abigail explained why she had come. She asked Mrs. Trudy if she would take care of the strangers.

"I certainly will not," Mrs. Trudy said sharply. "And you can tell your mother that I don't thank her for asking me. She's the preacher's wife. It's her place to take care of them."

"But our house is full, and Mother can't find a place to put even one more—" Abigail didn't have a chance to finish.

74

"I don't know these people. They're probably thieves or tramps. I wouldn't have a knife or spoon left in the house by morning. I won't take them in. Good night." Mrs. Trudy shut the door and left Abigail standing outside.

Abigail walked away out of sight. Then she stopped and stuck her tongue out at Mrs. Trudy's house. "Just wait till the next time you want me to do something for you," she said. "I won't run any more errands for you, you old witch. You're going to get the surprise of your life when you ask me!"

"Who were you talking to, Nabby?" asked Father. He had come up the hill just in time to see Abigail talking to herself.

Abigail jumped. She hadn't heard him coming. "I wasn't talking to anyone, but I wish I could tell Mrs. Trudy what I think of her. She's the meanest old thing in the world. I hate her."

"Oh, oh, Abigail. That's no way to talk."

"But, Father, just listen to what she did." Abigail told him what had happened. "I'm going to tell everybody in town just how mean she is."

"No, Abigail, that won't do at all. Just forget all about her. Don't even mention this to your mother. Let's talk about something else. Tell me how many people came today."

By the time she had counted all the callers, Abigail had forgotten Mrs. Trudy. "Now, you keep count on your fingers and let's see how many will be staying all night, Father," she said.

Then it was Father who wondered where they were going to put everybody. But he knew Mrs. Smith would manage. It had been this way before. Each time she made things come out right. Father knew she would do it again.

Tonight, though, Mother was at her wit's end. There wasn't another spot to put anyone else.

"Why can't Mary and I sleep in the attic with Phoebe?" asked Abigail.

"I hadn't thought of that," said Mother. "I don't know whether I should let you or not. You might catch cold." But before anyone could stop her, Abigail had Tom carry a straw mattress up and lay it next to Phoebe's by the chimney.

At bedtime Mother went up and tucked the girls in. It was cozy there. Strings of corn and peppers made a pretty screen for their bedroom. Walnuts and butternuts in baskets under the eaves gave it a spicy smell.

Mother took the candle away, and left the girls in the dark. Mary was asleep before Mother was downstairs. Abigail lay there listening. She kept hearing scurrying little sounds. She wondered if there were mice up here. "I wish I hadn't thought of sleeping here," she said. "I don't like the idea of mice running over my toes." She wiggled them to see if they were well covered.

Just then something grabbed her foot. "Eeek! Eeek!" she squealed.

"What's the matter?" cried Mary, waking from a sound sleep with a start.

"A rat or something's got me," cried Abigail. She kicked wildly.

"*Miaow!*" went the something. It was the cat. Phoebe brought it up to the garret now and then to keep mice away. It had seen Abigail's toes wiggling and had pounced on them.

Mary and Abigail began to giggle. They had a hard time stopping. Every time they thought of how Abigail squeaked, they started in again. Finally they settled down and slept, with the kitten at their feet.

Mary and Abigail used the garret after that whenever the rooms downstairs were crowded.

Of course Mrs. Trudy heard where they were sleeping. She was a little ashamed of herself then. She told Mother she would help out sometime. "I just want to be sure the right kind of people come to my house," she said.

All this company made a lot of extra work. Phoebe couldn't begin to do it by herself. Mary and Abigail had to help in the kitchen with the cooking and dishwashing and baking. They helped serve the meals. They looked after the smaller children. Mother had never been so busy. There wasn't time for lessons, or sewing or knitting, or even for talks about manners.

Abigail liked all this excitement. "It's like living in the meetinghouse," she said. "We don't have to go any place to hear what's going on. It's all happening right here in our own house."

Mother was worried though. "Abigail's getting too thin. She's working too hard."

Father was worried, too. "I think we'd better send Abigail away for a while," he said. "It isn't the work that I'm anxious about. There's a lot of sickness in the town. I didn't want to tell you, but a terrible throat disease has broken out. It doesn't seem to hurt grownups, but children are dying with it. Benjie Bicknell has it. So does Mrs. Burrell's little girl, Prudence. There's no telling when some of the children staying here might catch it. Then Abigail would be sure to take it just when she's feeling better."

"I'll send Nabby to her Grandmother Quincy," Mrs. Smith said. "Tom can take her over tomorrow morning."

Abigail and Grandmother Quincy

THE MINUTE Abigail heard that she was going on a long visit to her Grandmother Quincy's, she began to pack. She dragged out a big wooden sea chest.

"You won't need anything so big as that," said Mother. "You don't have very many clothes."

"Oh, yes, I will," said Abigail. "I'll show you." She was as busy as a bee running back and forth, getting all her things together.

"Now, Mother, come and see," she called after awhile. Mother looked and the box was brimful.

"Why, Nabby, what are you taking?" Mother was sure Abigail's clothes wouldn't half fill it.

"I have my Sunday dress and my petticoats and my new shoes and my bonnet and my shawl."

"What are all these other things?" Mother pulled out a box filled with straw, and a gunny sack full of cracked corn, and a bag of bran.

"Those are presents I'm taking to Grandmother," said Abigail. She hurriedly packed them back in the chest. "I'm giving her my baby chicks. The box with the straw is to carry them in. Of course I can't pack them till the last thing. The rest is feed for them."

"But, Nabby, you can't pack chickens. They'd smother before you arrived at Grandmother's. Besides, you don't have to take any presents."

"You always do," said Abigail. "The last time you went to Aunt Elizabeth's in Boston, you took a whole barrel full of things."

"But that was different," said Mother. "Your aunt lives in town. She doesn't have pigs and cows and sheep."

82

"You took her so many things," said Abigail.

"I took her some sausage and butter and beef and things that are hard to get there. In exchange, she gives me spices and dyes and cloth and needles and pins. Those are things I can't buy in the country. Grandmother has a barn lot full of chicks. She doesn't need any more."

Abigail was disappointed. "I can't go on a visit without some kind of present. Grandmother always brings me something."

"I'm too busy to help you, Nabby," said Mother. "Maybe you'll think of something before it's time to leave."

The next morning Abigail still hadn't thought of a present. "Why don't you give Grandmother the sampler you just finished?" asked Mother.

"That's too little," Abigail said unhappily.

"I think it would make a very nice present," Mother said. "It's the prettiest one you ever made. There's not a crooked stitch in it."

There wasn't time for Abigail to think of anything else, so she put the sampler in with her things. Tom strapped the big chest in the back of the cart. Mother had let her take it, after all. Father lifted the little girl up to the seat. Tom cracked the whip. The horse leaped forward, and down the hill they went.

The neighbors ran out and called good-by as the cart passed by. Benjie Bicknell saw Abigail from his window and waved. She saw him, too. She stood up and waved and cried, "Get well quick, Benjie!"

"Careful, Miss Nabby," said Tom. "Don't you fall." That reminded Abigail that she wasn't being ladylike, so she sat down, and only bowed to her other friends.

It was a fine day, and the road was dry. The four miles to Grandmother Quincy's rolled by swiftly. Abigail had often gone to the Quincy Homestead, which was called Mount Wollaston.

She knew just where the road turned and came out along the sea. Sometimes she could see ships in the distance. She knew, too, when they came to the beginning of Grandfather's farmland. She waved at the men working in the stone quarry on his place. They waved back.

"There goes the Reverend Smith's little daughter Nabby," one said. "It'll be lonesome back at the parsonage without her."

Finally Tom turned off the road into the lane that led around the hill to Grandmother's house. This was the first time Abigail had come here alone. She felt important when the cart whirled up to the front steps of the fine, big house. Grandfather and Grandmother were waiting for her. They hugged her and lifted her to the ground.

Tom unstrapped the chest. He hoisted it to his shoulder and carried it into the house.

"Why, what a big box for such a little girl!" said Grandmother.

"I have a present in it for you," said Abigail. She could hardly wait to get into the house to unpack. Grandmother pretended not to notice how little there was in the chest. She was pleased with the sampler.

"I wanted to bring you something big and important." Abigail told Grandmother about the chicks and how disappointed she was to give her a little thing like a sampler.

"I like the sampler much better, though," said Grandmother. "It's something you made yourself. It's a better present than a whole chest full of dead chickens, don't you think?"

Abigail nodded. She was a little ashamed now of her big ideas.

"It isn't how much a thing costs or how large it is that counts," said Grandmother. "I am pleased that you wanted to give me something. That is what is important. Whenever I look at the sampler, I shall think of you."

She put the sampler on the candle table by the front door, so that everyone would see it.

Something about Grandmother made it easy to tell her things. She and Abigail were still unpacking the chest when Abigail told her what Mother had said about being a young lady. "It's going to be hard to remember not to run and skip," she said. "But the hardest part will be to sit at home and wait till the men come and tell me what's happening. That isn't fair. I can't do anything brave and important and be a lady."

"You're wrong about that, Nabby," said Grandmother. "Women do things that are as brave as anything men do, but we don't hear about them. You'll see that I'm right if you keep your eyes and ears open. Now let's go down to dinner. Grandfather Quincy is waiting."

"I've never seen women doing any brave things," Abigail said doubtfully. "I suppose I'll have to be a lady whether it's any fun or not."

"It's easy to be a lady here at your house," Abigail told Grandmother a few months later.

She was watching Grandmother serve tea. The maid had set the best tea things on the table. Grandmother was wearing her prettiest lace cap and her silk dress. She poured the tea and Abigail handed the cups around. Then Abigail passed the wafers and cake. She curtsied at each chair. It was an elegant tea party. It was a quiet party, too, because there wasn't anyone there but Abigail and her grandmother. Abigail was practicing being a lady.

"You did everything perfectly today, Nabby," said Grandmother. "The Queen of England couldn't have had a nicer tea than this. After you go home, you must keep on doing this. No matter how busy your mother is, ask her to sit down while you serve tea to her and your father and his guests. All of them will profit by having a little time to rest and talk."

"It won't be like this, though," said Abigail. "We don't have pretty china cups or a silver teapot. And Mother won't have time to put on her best dress and her Sunday cap."

"It doesn't make any difference whether you serve with a cracked bowl or a golden teapot. If you are pleasant and have nice manners you can make a party out of very simple things."

Abigail promised that she would try. The summer was nearly over and soon she would go home. No more children were getting the throat disease. The new meetinghouse was ready. And Mother had sent word she couldn't spare Abigail any longer. They were too lonesome without her at the parsonage.

"I'll have lots to show everyone when I get home," said Abigail. "Grandfather asked me to read to him every morning out of his books, and I can read almost anything now. Father will be pleased at that."

"You have learned many other things too," said Grandmother Quincy.

"I know I have. I've learned all kinds of new embroidery stitches. I can bake a yellow cake that is almost as good as mother's. I've lots and lots of stories to tell Mary and Will, too. I'll never forget this summer, Grandmother, and I'm going to surprise the family."

Abigail was right. Everyone was surprised at all she had learned while she was gone. There was one thing she hadn't mentioned, though, that Mother noticed first of all. She talked to Father about it.

"Abigail is growing up. She isn't a tomboy any more. It doesn't seem possible she could have changed so in one summer."

"I don't want her to change too much," said Father. "She wouldn't be Nabby without her friendly, bright ways."

"She'll always keep those," said Mother.

90

Abigail's Fortune

IT WAS wash day. Mother called to Tom early, as soon as she saw the weather was going to be clear. She told him to fill the big iron kettle with water and start a fire under it in the yard.

"We can't count on many more days like this before winter sets in," she said. "We'd better wash the sheets, quilts, and blankets, as well as the other clothes."

"Oh, dear," Abigail groaned to Mary. "That means I'll have to do the kitchen work. I wish I could go to school like you, and get out of scouring pots and pans. While you're having fun with the other children, I'll be scouring away."

The girls were dressing. Mary put on her school clothes. Abigail picked out the shabbiest dress she had.

"School isn't much fun," Mary said. "The best part is when it's out and we're on our way home. Do you have to wear that old dress, Nabby? It makes you look so thin."

"There's no use wearing my second best to scour in. I know that's what I'll have to do." Abigail went downstairs looking sad and tired. She made everybody else feel sad, just to look at her. She wished she was back at Grandmother Quincy's, where there was more help.

"Doesn't Nabby have a prettier dress to wear around the house?" asked Father. "It seems to me she has worn that one for years."

"Of course she has something better," said Mother. "But Nabby's very sensible to wear her old dress. She's going to polish the pewter and scour the kettles today."

Abigail looked at Mary as if to say, "I told you so. I knew I'd have to do it."

"Can't Phoebe do that part of the work?" Father asked. Abigail cheered up a little.

"We're washing this morning," said Mother, "and it's all two people can do to lift heavy wet bedcovers and stretch them to dry properly. Phoebe can't do everything."

Father said no more.

"If we are through before noon, I want to take Elizabeth and Nabby to Hingham this afternoon when you go. I'll visit with my sister Anna while you go to the horse fair," said Mother.

Then Abigail felt quite happy again. She hurried through breakfast so she could get to her work. She wanted to be finished in time to go to Aunt Anna's house.

Mary and Will went off to school. Mary was thirteen now, Abigail was eleven, Will was nine and little Elizabeth was five.

Abigail began on the pots and pans first. She saved the pewter till the last. She didn't really mind doing it, because it looked so pretty when it was finished.

Then things began to happen. The fine wood ashes she was scouring with made her sneeze. They always did.

"Oh, Nabby, you're taking cold," Mother said. "I'm afraid you'd better not go with us this afternoon. It's colder than it looks, and you might get sick. We want very much to keep you from getting even one cold this winter."

Abigail tried to tell Mother that it was only the ashes, but that didn't do any good. Mother said this was the way Abigail's winter colds always began. She must stay inside the rest of the day.

Then Mother asked her to help Elizabeth get ready. Elizabeth was as lively as a cricket. Abigail had a hard time making her stand still long enough to dress her.

The washing was done, dinner was over, and Mother was ready to leave, when something else happened. Phoebe got a crick in her back. "You probably were chilled while you were working outside," Mother said. "You'd better go right to bed. Now you just rest and keep warm, and don't you worry about a thing."

She helped Phoebe to her garret room. She told Abigail to run up in a little while and see how the old woman was getting along. "The soup and dumplings for supper are on the fire," she said as she went out. "Just see that the kettle doesn't boil over. I'm sorry you can't go with us, dear, but it *is* getting colder. And it's just as well someone can be here with Phoebe. She's getting old and we must take care of her."

Abigail watched them drive off. She tried to look cheerful, but inside she was as blue as she could be. It seemed as if everyone always had fun but her. Would it always be this way?

She started polishing the pewter. As she worked, she talked to herself. "You're not well enough to go visiting, Nabby," she said, imitating Mother's voice. "But you can scrub and scour, and look after the children, and cook the dinner and run up and downstairs to look after Phoebe. All that won't hurt you."

The more she talked, the angrier she got. The angrier she got, the harder she rubbed the pewter. At last she twisted the handle right off the water pitcher!

"Oh, bother, anyway!" Abigail cried. "Everything's gone wrong all day." She shook the pitcher and threw the handle on the floor. "Go on and break. See if I care! Nobody cares how I feel. I even have to wait on the hired help."

Abigail was ashamed of herself as soon as she said that. "Poor old Phoebe. She's always been so good to me. I wonder if it's warm enough for her up in the garret."

Abigail had been sitting back in the chimney corner. It was nice and warm there, but the rest of the room felt chilly. "It must be lots colder," she thought. The wind was blowing a gale. It howled around the house. "I'd better run up to the attic to see how Phoebe is."

Abigail could see her breath as she went up the stairs. "It's too cold up here for you, Phoebe," she said. "You'll have to let me help you down to my room. It's warm there."

No, Phoebe wouldn't hear of such a thing. "I won't have you waiting on me and I won't take your bed. I'm all right here."

"I'll be sure to catch cold if I come up here," said Abigail, "and you know you'll have to have a little care."

In that case Phoebe said she'd come down. Abigail pulled one of the trundle beds in her room close to the fire. Soon the poor old woman was warm and comfortable.

Abigail built up the fires in her room and the kitchen. "I wonder what that noise is outdoors," she said, in a little while. "I've heard it for some time. It sounds like cows bawling." Suddenly she realized that was exactly what it was. "There's something wrong with the cattle! I'd better go see about them."

She opened the door. The wind was so strong it blew her backward. It was a cold wind, too. No wonder the cattle were lowing. They knew there was danger in the air.

Abigail threw all her weight behind the door and slammed it shut between gusts. Then she went upstairs to Phoebe. "Do you hear the cows? Don't you think it means they should be let into the barn?"

"The wind is moaning and whining around the house. That means a storm is close," Phoebe said. "The sooner the cows are in the barn the better. If we wait till your father and Tom get back it may be too late. But I'm afraid for you to go out alone. I ought to go with you."

"I'll take Rover," said Abigail. "I'm sure we can manage. Don't worry about us."

She put on all the clothes she could wear. She looked as round as a butterball. "Here, Rover," she called. The dog ran with her to the pasture.

It was not so hard going because the wind was with them. Coming back to the barn was a different matter. There were times when Abigail had to drop on her hands and knees to keep from being blown off her feet. But she made it. Rover herded the cows into the barn lot and Abigail shut them in. She shook down plenty of hay for them and closed everything up tight.

The little girl started back to the house, but Rover wouldn't go in with her. He stood and barked. "You're trying to tell me something. What is it? Do you want to go after Mary and Will? Is that what you mean?"

But Abigail knew that the schoolmaster wouldn't let the children come home if a storm was close. She tried to tell Rover they were safe. He kept on whining and barking.

"I know what's the matter!" cried Abigail at last. "The sheep! We've got to get the sheep!"

When she said "sheep," Rover raced for the hillside. He knew as well as Abigail that the sheep didn't have much sense. They weren't like the cows. They would be caught far from shelter by the storm, and they might freeze.

The sky was growing darker, and the wind was colder. Abigail felt it through all the clothes she was wearing. Rover was a wise old fellow. He soon had the sheep headed toward the barn. They reached it just ahead of the storm. Snow began to fall as Rover drove the sheep into the shed, and Abigail closed the door.

"Now back to the house!" cried Abigail. She was shivering by this time.

The snow fell so fast she couldn't see a thing. Not a fence post or tree trunk or bush told her where she was. She took a good hold of Rover's collar and counted on him to guide her. It was only a short distance, but if it hadn't been for the dog, she could not have found her way. As it was, she had her head down and rammed right into the house. It didn't hurt her because of the heavy shawl over her head, but it surprised her. She was glad to be back, anyway.

How warm and cheerful and bright the kitchen looked! Phoebe had been so frightened when she saw the snow begin to fall before Abigail returned that she had come downstairs. She was wrapped up ready to go out and hunt her.

"Phoebe, you're standing up straight! What about your back?"

"I was so worried about you I forgot all about it." Phoebe started to put the supper on the table. "I'm all right now."

"Isn't it too early to eat? Father and Mother will be late. Shouldn't we wait for them?"

"They won't try to get home tonight," Phoebe said. "That would be foolish. They know we're safe. Your father had Tom fill all the wood boxes before he left, and pile more wood at the back door. He brought fresh water from the well, too. Your mother knows there's plenty of food in the house. There's no need for them to risk coming home through the storm."

"How about Will and Mary?" asked Abigail.

"They'll have a good time at the schoolhouse. The teacher's home is in back of the schoolroom. His mother is a wonderful cook. She'll take good care of the children."

It was cozy, eating supper by the fire. It was a little lonesome, too. "It doesn't seem like the same house with only two of us, does it?" said Abigail. "It's nice to have all the family here. But it's good to know they're safe."

Phoebe didn't answer. She was looking at the tea leaves in her cup.

"Why are you doing that?" Abigail asked.

"Oh, when I was a girl, we used to read our fortunes in the tea leaves." Phoebe laughed. "It was silly of us, but it was fun."

"What does your fortune say?"

"Just the same thing. I'm going to be an old maid, and I'm going to stay right here in Weymouth. One good thing, though. The leaves promise I'll have better health for a while."

"Here, read mine, too," said Abigail.

Phoebe held the cup so the firelight shone on the leaves in the bottom. "My, my!" she cried. "Miss Nabby, you're going to be a fine lady. You'll be dressed in silks and satins. We won't see much of you around here. That's what the leaves say. You'll meet all kinds of great folk, and live in big cities. You're going to cross the ocean someday, too."

"You must be mistaken," Abigail said. "I don't want to cross the ocean, ever. Ships are too leaky and the waves too high. Besides, I'll never go anywhere. Something always keeps me at home. I can't even get as far as Hingham."

"You will, though," said Phoebe, wagging her head. "People are going to know you all over the world. You won't always stay home."

Abigail thought this was a good joke. She laughed merrily. So did Phoebe. They drank some more tea and read their fortunes again. This time Phoebe showed Abigail how to read them. They were having such a good time they couldn't believe the clock when it struck eight.

"We'd better get to bed," said Phoebe. "We're using up a lot of wood."

She banked the kitchen fire with ashes and let Abigail lead the way upstairs with the candle. They pulled Abigail's trundle bed close to the fire, too, and piled on extra covers.

Abigail was about to drop off to sleep when she remembered the water pitcher. "I'll see if Toby's father can fix the handle for me," she thought. "It's too bad I was so cross and unhappy. I'll try not to be like that again."

Everybody was back before noon the next day. The snow had stopped falling as suddenly as it began, and the wind had blown it off the road. The drifts weren't too deep for the cart.

"Drive as fast as you dare, Tom," Father had said. He was anxious to get home.

He could hardly believe his eyes when he saw that the cows and sheep were all safe in the barn. When Phoebe told him how Abigail had done it, he praised his little girl.

"I can always count on Nabby," he said. "If there's something that has to be done, she'll see that it's done, or do it herself."

Off to Boston!

"IT'S TIME to get up, Abigail," said Mary early one morning. "You haven't forgotten we're going to Boston today, have you?"

"No," said Abigail, but she didn't get up. She kept her eyes tightly closed.

"You aren't sick, are you?" Mary asked anxiously. "You will be able to go with us, won't you. I don't want you to miss the trip."

"No, I was just trying to guess what the weather's like. I hope it's good."

"I can tell you without guessing," said Mary. "It's cold! The floor is like ice, and the window's covered with frost."

"Good! Then I'll get up," said Abigail, hopping out of bed. "It can't rain if it's frosty. Mother said we couldn't go if it rained. I was afraid to look out the window."

She began to dress in a hurry. "Now if I just don't sneeze or sniffle before we start . . ." she said hopefully to herself.

The Smiths were going to visit Uncle Isaac and Aunt Elizabeth. Uncle Isaac was Father's brother. He was a merchant and had a store and warehouse in Boston. He owned ships that sailed all over the world for goods.

The day before he had sent word to Father that one of the ships had just come into the harbor. It was one of his finest ships, and it carried a very rich cargo.

"Come make us a visit and bring all the family," Uncle Isaac wrote. "It will be a fine time for the womenfolk to shop." Mother had begun to get ready at once.

This morning Abigail fairly held her breath until starting time. But nothing unlucky happened. They all set off bright and early. At the town of Braintree, Grandmother and Grandfather Quincy, Uncle John Norton and Aunt Anna joined them.

"The Hancocks and the Warrens and the Tufts are going, too," said Grandmother. "They'll be waiting at Roxbury." It made a long line of carts going to Boston. Uncle Isaac had sent word to as many good friends as he could reach. They would all be welcome.

Tom went ahead of the whole party with the wagon. It was filled with baggage and articles Mother was going to exchange at the market. Behind him came Father, driving the Smiths' carriage, and last came Uncle John. They set out at a good trot. On the way they came to a stretch of road that was wide enough for two carriages. Father pulled his to a stop.

"See that oak tree with the limb that reaches out over the road?" he asked when Uncle John had come alongside. Uncle John did.

"We'll race you to it," cried Father.

"Let's go!" Uncle John cried. With a crack of the whip, they were off. Uncle John pulled ahead at the start.

Father held his horse back a little. "I want to feel him out a bit," he said. This was a horse he had bought in a trade the day before. "I think he has plenty of speed and endurance."

Abigail was afraid Father wouldn't let the horse go fast enough. The oak tree was getting pretty close.

Uncle John looked back at Father and waved his whip and laughed with joy. "I'm afraid you got stung yesterday, Reverend," he shouted.

Father only grinned, but Abigail noticed he leaned forward and spoke to the horse and loosened the reins a little.

All at once the horse seemed to be flying over the ground. Uncle John looked back and saw the Smiths coming up fast. He whipped up his horse, but it didn't do any good. Father's horse went by so swiftly that Uncle John's horse seemed to be standing still.

Abigail waved saucily as they left the others behind. "I love to win," she said.

When Uncle John came up to them after the race was over, she was sorry she had acted so smart, because Cousin Johnnie and her brother Will were ready to cry. They had wanted to win as much as Abigail did.

"Oh, oh, oh," called Uncle John when he saw their faces, "we must be good sports. Everyone can't win. Coming home we'll try again. I'll handle the horse differently next time. We'll give 'em a good race then." The boys felt all right again. They were sure their horse would win the next race.

"I want to drive to the wharf," Father called to the cart behind, as they neared the city. "Isaac will probably be down there with the ship." The others decided they would go with him.

Soon wheels were rattling over the cobblestone street beside the wharf. Abigail liked this part of Boston. She had come here before with her aunt and uncle, when she visited them.

"Look at all the ships!" she cried. "I don't remember ever seeing so many in the bay at once. Oh, I wish I could sail across the ocean sometime, but I suppose I never will. I wish I was on the deck right now!"

"The whole whaling fleet is here," said Mary. "That's why there are so many ships. Look at all those flags flying. Isn't the harbor beautiful? I'd like to look at it all day."

"Out there beyond the fishing boats I see the *New Bethel*," said Abigail.

"Where? Where?" asked Mary eagerly.

The *New Bethel* was the name of their Cousin Edmund's ship. The girls always watched for it. They never forgot it had once captured a Spanish pirate ship with over a hundred chests of gold and silver in its hold.

"Where is Uncle Isaac's ship?" asked Mary.

"I don't see it," Abigail replied. "I hope we're in time to watch the crew unload. Maybe they brought in a ship full of gold and silver, too. Wouldn't it be exciting to watch them pour bag after bag of gold and silver into great chests— enough so you could bury your hands in gold?"

They were so busy looking for their uncle's boat and pointing out other ships that they didn't notice what was going on right in front of them.

Suddenly the coach stopped with a jerk. Two sailors, with long knives flashing, blocked the road. Two more held the horse's head.

"What does this mean?" asked Father. "Take your hands off my horse," he ordered sternly.

Abigail was proud of the way Father spoke. She, herself, was afraid. The men looked rough, like pirates, with rings in their ears and daggers in their bright sashes. What would they do to Father? Would they take him away?

"Oh, it's you, Reverend Smith," they said politely. They stepped back out of the way. "We're from the crew of your brother's ship. They're unloading now. The cargo is precious and they didn't want many strangers on the docks. Of course it's quite all right for you to be here." They let the carts through.

As they pulled away, the fiercest of the sailors called out, "Hello, Miss Nabby."

Abigail's mouth dropped open. "Why, it's Toby!" she exclaimed. "I didn't know you were on Uncle's ship. What did you bring home that is so precious? Gold?"

"No." Toby laughed. "Dyes, mostly. I'll show you some later."

116

Soon they came to the place where Uncle Isaac Smith's ship was docked. The members of the crew were working furiously. Some hoisted goods from the hold. Some loaded wheelbarrows, and wheeled them down the gangplank and up the street to the warehouse. Still others stood guard at all the roads. They stopped everyone who came out on the wharf.

"I didn't know dyes were precious," said Abigail. "Our pot of indigo blue just stands in the chimney corner most of the time. No one seems to notice it, except when Elizabeth spills some."

"That's because everyone has indigo," said Mary. "It isn't like the dyes in Uncle's ship. They are reds and yellows. They say the red is worth more than gold or jewels, because it's so hard to get."

Abigail craned her neck to see what the dye looked like. She wanted to ask Father to stop, but Mother shook her head.

117

"This is no place for women and children," she said. "We'll go straight to the warehouse. We'll rest in your uncle's office while the men watch the unloading. Tomorrow when things are settled down, we'll come to see the goods in the shops."

"But we'll miss all the fun that way," cried Abigail, disappointed. "I want to see everything today, while the men are hurrying about. I like to hear them shouting and singing."

"It isn't ladylike, Nabby, even to want to be in the midst of all this hurly-burly."

Abigail said no more. Mother wouldn't understand. Soon they were at the warehouse. Uncle Isaac was standing at the door waiting for them. The men helped the ladies from the carts.

Aunt Elizabeth was there. "I knew the menfolk would come straight here. I thought we might as well be shopping while they're sightseeing. I know they'll be on the wharf."

For a little while Abigail's spirits rose. Maybe she could go out on the docks after all. She was mistaken. The ship's clerks brought samples of all the things to the office. Mother and Grandmother and Aunt Anna and Aunt Elizabeth and their friends ordered what they wanted.

"This is much better than going to the shops," said Mother. "It's not nearly so tiring."

Abigail didn't think so. Her mind was out where things were going on.

Little Elizabeth soon tired of just looking, too. While the ladies were admiring silver teapots, and china and silks and laces, she began to play hide-and-seek with Abigail. She ducked behind the big sea chest in the corner, and under the tables piled with dress materials. Abigail pretended to have a hard time finding her. After a while they went out into the big storeroom where there were boxes and barrels of spices and coffee and tea. These gave them lots of hiding places.

The children played at one end of the room, out of the way of the men. Abigail had to watch her active little sister closely to keep track of her and to keep her from getting hurt.

They were having a good time, when all at once Elizabeth darted out of the warehouse into the street. Abigail ran after her. She knew Mother would be angry if they played outside. But before she could reach the door, Elizabeth had turned a corner and run up another street.

Abigail couldn't see her. She didn't know which way to turn. Most of the streets were narrow and winding. Some were lined on both sides with small warehouses. Near the wharf they opened to the fish market. Elizabeth could be hiding almost anywhere.

Abigail called into each open door as she went by. "Have you seen my sister Elizabeth? Did a little girl in a blue dress and white apron pass this way in the last few minutes?"

120

The men in each placed looked up, surprised. They weren't used to seeing well-dressed little girls playing around the wharf.

"No, miss," they all said. They all dropped their work and went out to stare after Abigail.

She had been searching only a few minutes, but it was long enough for her to be frightened. "What'll I do? Where shall I look next? Elizabeth is getting farther away from me every second." Then she caught a glimpse of Toby.

"Toby!" she called out, and ran to him. "I can't find Elizabeth." She explained how she had lost sight of the child.

"We'll find her," said Toby, "but we'll need help. There are too many places here to hide for only two of us to search." He ran to the guard at the nearest corner. "Beat a warning on your drum," he said. "Isaac Smith's little niece is lost."

The guard had a drum slung over his shoulder. He began to beat it with might and main.

Everywhere sailors dropped whatever they were doing, drew their knives, and came roaring to the drummer. The yells they let out sent chills up and down Abigail's back.

Toby shouted to them that Isaac Smith's niece was lost. Abigail was afraid the sailors would be angry when they learned that only a little girl was lost, but they weren't at all.

"We'll find her for you, Miss Nabby," they said. They put away their knives, and scattered in every direction. They went, two by two, up and down each street, stopping at every door, hunting behind every barrel and box.

Toby found Elizabeth after a little while, quite close to the warehouse. She had grown tired of waiting for Abigail and climbed into a wheelbarrow to rest. Toby carried her to Uncle Isaac's office. Father, Uncle John, and Uncle Isaac had gone there as soon as they heard the drum. They thought there was a riot.

The three men had rushed to the office to protect the women and children. They were relieved to see Abigail and Elizabeth and to learn that nothing serious had happened.

The drum beat again to tell the sailors that the little girl was found, and Toby was rewarded. Uncle Isaac ordered a fine suit of the best wool to be made for him.

Mother said, "How did you get your dress so dirty, Elizabeth? You look as if you had been sitting on the floor."

"I expect it's some of the dyestuff from the ship," said Toby.

"Dyestuff!" exclaimed Abigail. "I didn't see any. I wanted to see it."

"Why, you looked right at a wheelbarrow full of it," said Toby. "Elizabeth was resting on top."

Abigail was disgusted. Here she had wanted to see what dye looked like and had stared at a load of it without knowing it.

"It didn't look any different from chests of tea or spices," she said.

"You can't always judge the value of a thing by its looks," said Father, smiling.

"From the looks of Elizabeth's dress, I'd better get her to the house," Mother said.

"Oh! It's past dinnertime," cried Aunt Elizabeth. "We'll have to hurry. My cook is touchy about serving late, and good cooks are scarce in Boston. I couldn't replace her."

They all took their places quickly in the carts and drove away from the wharf to Uncle Isaac's and Aunt Elizabeth's house.

Abigail's Nightmare

EVERY TIME Abigail came to Aunt Elizabeth's she thought, "This is where I'd like to live always." She didn't know what she liked best about the house. Sometimes she thought it was all the servants. There were maids who cleaned the upstairs rooms. They also helped the ladies dress and curled their hair. Other maids looked after the downstairs, and certain ones served in the dining room. There were two menservants, a cook, and a butler.

Mary and Abigail always had the same room when they came to visit. They thought it was the prettiest one in the house.

They never ceased to admire the enormous feather bed with silk and lace curtains and coverlets. They loved to sit in the alcove, which had a little fireplace, a desk, and a chair. They spent hours there, writing letters.

Abigail liked another thing at Aunt Elizabeth's. They used lots of candles at night. She remembered the first time she had come here. She had thought the house was on fire, it was so bright. At home the Smiths burned only the candles they needed, because they made their own, and it was hard work. Here candles were everywhere—in brackets against the wall, in candlesticks on the mantels and candle tables, and in the crystal chandeliers in the two living rooms. It looked like fairyland when they were all alight.

"It gives you more time to read, when you have light at night," Abigail said. "Yet people here don't read as much as we do at home."

There was always company. Captains from ships came, and merchants, doctors, and lawyers. All of them had stories to tell. Listening to them was better than reading any books.

There was more company than usual this night. Uncle Isaac's friends came to tell him how glad they were his ship had reached port.

Mary and Abigail sat in the chimney corner in the living room and listened. They were so afraid they would miss a word that at times they scarcely breathed. The captains told tales of outwitting pirates. They told of narrow escapes from terrible storms that tossed ships as if they were eggshells. The men from the fishing fleet told of fights with Indians, and hardships in the frozen North.

Abigail felt as if she were out in the midst of these adventures herself. She jumped when someone laid a hand on her shoulder. "Time to go to bed," Mother whispered.

Abigail drew a deep breath. It was like waking up from a dream to look around and find she was still in Aunt Elizabeth's parlor. She would have liked to stay to hear one more story, but she knew better than to ask. The girls were not often allowed to stay downstairs this late. So they slipped out quietly and went up to their own pretty room. Soon they were sound asleep.

Abigail didn't sleep so well as usual. She had had too much excitement during the day, and she had nightmares. One in particular was the craziest ever. She dreamed that a big bull from the pasture in Weymouth was up here in her bedroom at Aunt Elizabeth's.

"How did *you* get to Boston?" she asked. The bull just looked at her. "How did you get up the stairs? You don't belong in here. You're too big. You'll break the mirror!" she scolded.

The bull kept turning around, knocking into things and breaking them.

"Look out!" Abigail cried in her dream.

"You're moving the bed, and bumping into the china cupboard. You'll break my teapot."

The china cupboard was the one that belonged in the kitchen at home. Yet here it was in a Boston bedroom. And in it was a beautiful teapot she had seen in Uncle Isaac's office that morning. Somehow or other it belonged to Abigail now. She had admired it greatly.

The bull's tail was swishing things off the desk. It sent the candlestick flying. It struck the teapot and knocked it onto the floor. It fell with a loud crash.

This was more than Abigail could stand. "Get out!" she screamed. She shoved against the bull with all her weight.

"Nabby, Nabby, you're pushing me out of bed!" cried Mary. "Move over!"

Abigail woke with a start. "I was trying to get that bull out of here."

130

"Bull!" shrieked Mary. "Where?"

Abigail looked around. She was still in Aunt Elizabeth's house. There was no bull. There was no cupboard.

"I guess I was dreaming," she said. Then she grabbed Mary and held onto her for dear life. "What's happening?" she cried.

Mary held onto Abigail, too. The bed really was moving. That great big feather bed was waltzing around the room. Chairs were rocking, pictures were falling off the walls. The candlesticks fell to the floor.

They heard Father pounding on their door. "Are you all right, children? We're having an earthquake. Don't be frightened. I'm right here, and nothing is going to hurt you."

The earthquake lasted several minutes. "There won't be a single pretty thing left," Abigail thought. "Everything will be broken." But there was surprisingly little damage.

Many dishes were broken, and the clock on the stairs stopped and wouldn't run again.

"No one was hurt," Father said when it was over. "That's the thing that really matters."

Everyone got up and dressed and went downstairs. They all talked at once, telling how queer they had felt during the earthquake. Someone pounded hard on the front door. It was the night watchman. He nearly yanked the doorknocker from its socket.

"Please look at your fireplaces, Mr. Smith," he said. "A lot of chimneys have been shaken down all over town. Several houses are on fire. Is everything all right here?"

"No one seems to be hurt," said Uncle Isaac.

"You'd better count noses to be sure," the watchman said. "Is anyone missing?"

Uncle Isaac began to call names. The Tufts, the Quincys, the Warrens, the John Nortons, the William Smiths—all said "Here, here."

"But where's little Will?" Father asked.

No one had seen Will. They shouted his name. There was no answer.

Everybody tramped up into Will's room. There was no sign of him. Abigail saw part of the counterpane hanging down under the bed.

She tried to lift it off the floor. It was heavy. She gave it a good pull, and out rolled Will. He had fallen out of bed without waking. All he did now was to rub his eyes and climb back in again.

The next morning he didn't remember a thing about the earthquake. He wouldn't believe there had been one until he went outdoors.

Other people weren't so lucky as Uncle Isaac. Trees had fallen on roofs and smashed them in. Falling bricks had injured men and women.

The worst damage was at the docks. Waves had dashed the ships into one another. Some were lifted up and crushed against the wharf. Warehouses were knocked down.

Tea, coffee, spices, and dyes were all jumbled together. Wine casks had split open and the wine ran in streams down the street or mixed with salt water. Priceless silks and laces were ruined by salt water or dyes. Beautiful silver and china articles were broken.

134

"It isn't so bad for me as it might have been, though," said Uncle Isaac. "If the men hadn't worked so hard and stored most of our cargo yesterday, we'd have been ruined. We were lucky that our warehouse wasn't smashed."

The captains whose ships had not been ruined by the earthquake helped those who had lost their vessels. Everyone said it was a miracle that the whaling fleet wasn't wiped out. It was far enough out in the bay not to be dashed to pieces.

The Smith's visit was spoiled. Father wanted to get home to see how Weymouth had come through the earthquake. Mother wanted to see how their house had stood it, and if Phoebe was all right. They packed and were ready to leave as soon as breakfast was over.

"Let Abigail stay here with me," begged Aunt Elizabeth. "She looks thin, and I think the air here is good for her. We'll bring her back when we come at Christmas time."

Father did not like to leave Abigail behind. He missed her so at home. But he wanted her to have some good times, too. He knew she was rather lonely in Weymouth. So often, when she planned an outing, she got sick or something happened that kept her at home. Even this visit to Boston had been cut short. He decided Abigail should have a holiday.

"Tom," he called, "pull Nabby's box out of the wagon. She's going to stay with her Aunt Elizabeth for a while."

Abigail didn't go home until Christmas. When they saw her they hardly knew her. She wasn't fat, but her cheeks were rosy, and her black eyes sparkled. She had some pretty new dresses. She was gay and happy.

"Why, Nabby Smith is a beautiful girl," said Mrs. Trudy. "I wonder what tonic her Aunt Elizabeth gave her. I must find out and give some to my little Silence."

136

But it wasn't the medicine her aunt had given Abigail that had done her so much good. It was the wonderful time she had, riding and visiting and hearing what was going on in the world.

Father was glad to see her so well and bright, but he was a little worried, too. He was afraid she would miss all the excitement of the city.

"Do you wish you were back in Boston?" he asked her one day.

"No, indeed, Father," she said. "No matter what we were doing, I missed you and Mother. There was another thing I missed. We went to fine churches in Boston, but I didn't hear one sermon that was half so good as yours."

Father laughed heartily at this, but his heart felt warm and proud.

Abigail's
Birthday Party

"You'll make yourself sick working so hard, Nabby," said Mary one day. "The rugs aren't really dirty. Let them go."

"No, indeed," Abigail said. "Every inch of this house is going to be scoured and cleaned. Not a single thing is to be missed." She was planning a party for her twelfth birthday. She had been getting ready for it for weeks.

It was to be the best party anyone in Weymouth had ever had. She was going to have wonderful new refreshments that no one there ever had had before. She was making cakes and candies from Aunt Elizabeth's recipes.

There was to be a knitting contest, too. Grandmother Quincy was giving a prize to the girl who could knit the fastest and neatest. Everyone was excited about it. The prize was a sewing case with a real gold thimble in it. All the girls in Weymouth were practicing every spare minute, hoping to win it.

"It's the prettiest sewing case I ever saw," said Abigail. "And the thimble is perfectly beautiful. You've just got to win it, Mary."

"I'm afraid Silence Trudy will, as usual," Mary said. "I almost wish it wasn't your party. Then you could be in the contest. I know you would win because you knit so well."

The day before the party everything was ready. The house was in shining order. The pots and pans hanging on the kitchen wall were like mirrors. The candlesticks, the andirons, the fire tongs, the teakettle and even the poker were polished. The rugs were spotless.

Abigail came downstairs singing. She was so happy she gave a little skip. Kerplop!

"What was that?" called Mother. "Is the cat in the cupboard again?"

"No," Abigail said, laughing merrily. "I dropped my book."

She had been going around the house balancing a book on her head to keep from getting round-shouldered.

She came in and sat by the fire with Mother and Grandmother Quincy and Mary and Elizabeth. They were all knitting.

"Why are you so happy?" Grandmother asked. "Has something good happened?"

"Oh, everything is perfect," Abigail answered. "I wish it could always be like this. The weather's nice. I'm well and I'm going to have a party. And Silence Trudy is sick and can't come. She's been out of school a whole week. She can't possibly get well in time."

"Why, Abigail," said Mother, "I'm ashamed of you. You're the last person in the world to be glad that anyone's sick. You know how disappointing it is to have to stay at home."

"But, Mother," said Mary, "you don't know how dreadful Silence is. Let me tell you what she did. You know we've been going to one another's house every afternoon to knit stockings for the soldiers at Fort Henry."

Mother knew about that. The girls had been knitting all summer.

"It's pretty boring just to sit there knitting every afternoon, so we started a contest," Abigail said. "Each day, when we've finished, we sew a little colored thread in the row where we leave off. Then we measure and see who has knit the most. Sometimes we have a little prize."

Grandmother nodded. "I know. That's what we used to do when I was a girl. Knitting mittens and stockings was fun in a contest."

141

"Well, this summer Silence has been winning nearly every time. It gets tiresome. We wouldn't mind if she didn't boast so much about it. Besides, Mary is really a better knitter and is just as fast. But she isn't any good in a contest. She gets nervous and drops stitches, or her yarn becomes tangled just because she is trying to win."

"Why don't *you* win, then?" asked Mother. "You're faster than Mary is."

"That's what makes us so angry," said Abigail. "When Silence saw that I could beat her, she went around in a sly way and got the girls to make a new rule. She said I could practice more than they did, because I was sick and didn't have to go to school. So they made a rule that you have to go to school to be counted in the contest."

"So Silence wins and wins," Mary added.

"And that's why I'm glad she's sick and can't come tomorrow. Because now Mary will win the thimble, and she deserves to."

142

"I think Silence is mean," said Elizabeth.

"You're all very foolish," said Mother. "You're thinking more of winning than of knitting stockings for the Weymouth men who are fighting the Indians up north. You should forgive Silence, Nabby, and not worry about who wins the prize. The important thing is that the soldiers who are fighting our battles in bitter cold weather keep as warm as possible."

"How can I forgive her, unless she changes her ways? She's as mean as her mother."

"You'll be much happier if you forgive her," said Grandmother. "Nothing can spoil your party if your conscience is clear."

"Nothing can spoil the party now, anyway," Abigail thought. Aloud she said, "I'll forgive Silence, especially since she's sick."

The next morning, Abigail changed her mind. In the first place, Mrs. Trudy came to borrow some sugar and some flour.

Of course Abigail and Mary knew she had come to snoop in the kitchen. She always liked to go around Weymouth and tell everyone ahead of time what was to be served. It made the girls cross when Mrs. Trudy came in and saw all the goodies spread out on the kitchen table.

"I don't see why you care," said Elizabeth. "What difference does it make if people know what they're going to eat?"

"I just wanted to get the best of Mrs. Trudy once," said Abigail.

"Oh, well," said Mary, "we still have Silence. She's the one I want to get even with. I don't care about her mother."

The time for the party finally came. The guests began to arrive. Every little girl in the town was invited. Of course the mothers came, too. They almost always came to the children's parties. Today they all wanted to watch the contest and sample Abigail's cooking at teatime.

144

There was a feeling of excitement as the girls took their places. The sewing case lay on the table where everyone could see it. Abigail could have hugged herself when she looked at it. It was so pretty, and the thimble fitted Mary exactly. Without Silence there, it was the same as if it were Mary's already.

Grandmother stepped to the middle of the room. She was to start the contest. Then Abigail heard a sound that made her heart turn over. Silence was at the door, laughing, and looking as well as ever.

"Hello, everybody," she called out.

It was all Abigail could do to speak politely to her, but somehow she managed.

"We just thought we'd surprise everyone," Mrs. Trudy simpered. "You were making such a secret of things, we decided to have a little secret too. Silence hasn't been ill at all. She was only resting so she could do her best today."

"We were just ready to begin," said Abigail. "You barely got here in time."

"Oh, they're in plenty of time to watch," said Grandmother Quincy.

"*I'll* watch, of course," said Mrs. Trudy, "but Silence will be in the contest."

"This is really too bad," said Grandmother. "Silence can't take part. You see, I am following the girls' rule that only those in school can enter the contest. That will leave Abigail and Silence out of it. The others are ready to begin."

Mrs. Trudy blinked in surprise. She looked as if there were many things she would like to say. But Grandmother Quincy was the leading lady of this part of the colony. People didn't speak hastily to her.

"That's a foolish rule, isn't it?" Grandmother Quincy asked. "I don't see why the girls ever made it in the first place."

Mrs. Trudy said she didn't either.

Several of the children spoke up. "Silence made us do it. It was her idea."

Silence and Mrs. Trudy grew red in the face.

"Let's go home, Mother," said Silence. "I know when I'm not wanted." The mother and daughter left, holding their heads high.

"Why did you make such a silly rule, anyway?" her mother asked on their way home.

Silence began to cry. "I felt I had to win over Nabby some way. She's so pretty and so smart. Everybody likes her. Nobody notices me."

Her mother said she deserved to lose.

No one at the party said anything. Grandmother waited to see what the girls would do.

"I feel sorry for Silence," said Abigail after a minute. "The contest isn't going to be so much fun without her somehow."

"That's the way I feel," Mary said. "The main thing was to try to win from her."

The other girls nodded.

"The rule didn't really mean you couldn't be in the contest if you were just absent from school a few days. Shall I go bring her back?" asked Abigail. "She was crying when she left, and she might cry all the afternoon. The contest means more to her than it does to the rest of us. She isn't a very happy person."

The girls all said, "Of course, if you really want to. It's your party."

"Will it be all right if I do, Grandmother?"

"Yes, run quickly." Grandmother had hoped this would happen.

Abigail popped out of the house and was down the hill after Mrs. Trudy and Silence in a hurry. "Mrs. Trudy! Silence!" she called.

They stopped and waited for her.

"Come back, Silence, and try to win. I told Grandmother the rule didn't count if you were only absent from school a few days. They're waiting for you."

148

"Abigail," said Mrs. Trudy, "you're very generous. Silence has told me how she started that rule. I don't know any other little girl who would be so kind as to give her another chance. If your grandmother will let you enter the contest, too, then I think it might be all right for Silence to be in it. Shall we go back and talk it over?"

That was what they did. Grandmother said, "You know that Abigail is likely to win, don't you, Silence? You still want her to be in the contest, knowing you may lose?"

"Yes, indeed," said Silence, "but I won't give up, Nabby. I'm going to knit just as fast as I can. You'll have to be better than you ever were to win, because I'm going to try my best."

Then, at the drop of Grandmother's handkerchief the race was on. The way the girls' fingers flew made the mothers dizzy. "No one can be so quick as Abigail," they said. Then, they said, "No one can be so quick as Silence."

150

The lead went back and forth. At first, Abigail seemed to be winning. Then Silence seemed to be ahead. The other girls soon dropped out. They couldn't keep up the pace those two set.

"Finished!"

Two voices rang out at the same second. It was a tie. It was impossible to say that one had been ahead of the other.

"Now what will you do, Mrs. Quincy?" asked one mother. "Draw straws? Have them do it over and over until somebody wins?"

"No," said Grandmother. "One contest is enough. Fortunately I had two sewing cases made. They're almost exactly alike. The only difference is I had Abigail's name engraved on the thimble of one. I meant to give it to her for a birthday present. I'm happy to give it to her now as a prize. And here on the table is the one for Silence. I am proud to give prizes to two little girls who can knit so well."

Silence was so happy she clapped her hands, and let out little squeals. "I'm so proud to win it," she cried. "I like it better since I won it fairly. Thank you so much, Mrs. Quincy. And thank you, Abigail, for letting me be in the contest. I'm sorry I acted so mean this summer."

"Grandmother," Abigail said that night, "you are right about forgiving people. I nearly spoiled my own party by hating Silence. The minute I ran after her, I felt much happier."

A Young Lady

IT WAS a bitter winter night. Everybody had gone to bed at the parsonage except Abigail. She was sitting by the fire in her bedroom writing a long letter to Silence Trudy. It was more than two years after the knitting contest. The girls had been good friends ever since that time.

"I wish you'd snuff out the candles and come to bed, Nabby," said Mary. "It's too cold for you to sit up. Besides, it's awfully late. Can't you finish in the morning?"

"I'll be through in a few minutes," said Abigail. "I'm all wrapped up, and I must get this letter off on the next post."

She blew on her fingers to warm them. Mary was right about the cold. Abigail was wrapped up in a blanket, and was sitting as close to the fire as she dared. Still she felt like a block of ice. The ink was almost freezing in her quill pen.

"No letter can be that important," said Mary a few minutes later. "What on earth do you find to write about?"

Abigail blushed. She and Silence made up things to write. They pretended they were great ladies who had all kinds of exciting adventures. Sometimes Abigail almost forgot the stories weren't real. Tonight she was so wrought up she couldn't sleep if she did go to bed.

"Nabby! What do you mean by staying up so late?" Mother had seen a light in the girls' room and come to see if anything was wrong. "You'll ruin your complexion, losing so much sleep," she scolded. "Your eyes will be red, and you'll probably get sick again, too."

154

Abigail put away her writing materials and went to bed at once. She went to sleep immediately and overslept the next morning.

Mother didn't like that. "I think I'd better put a stop to Nabby's letter writing," she said. "She loses too much sleep. It is foolish, anyway."

"No, no," said Father. "So often Nabby can't go to parties, or have the outdoor fun with her friends that Mary has. Writing to people takes the place of visiting with them. It keeps her from feeling lonely and left out of things. It's good for her. Let her go ahead with it."

So Abigail went on writing letters, not only to Silence but to all her friends. Her notes weren't always about make-believe happenings. There was so much going on in the next few years, she hardly took time to imagine things.

France and England were still at war. The Indians north of New England were on the side of the French.

They attacked and burned little frontier villages, and they killed men, women, and children. They took Fort Henry, where many Massachusetts boys were stationed. Not one captive was left alive. Some of Abigail's cousins were among the people killed.

Out at sea, French warships captured English fishing boats and cut off many merchant ships bringing supplies to the colonies. Hard times came for the people of Massachusetts. Their only food was what they raised on their farms. Their only clothes were those they made with the wool from their own sheep.

At the Smiths' home the girls were never idle. They spun and wove whenever there was a spare moment. As they worked they listened to the talk of the menfolk. It seemed to Abigail that all the news of the war was bad. "How long can it last?" she wondered. "Why doesn't England send soldiers to fight the Indians?"

"England is a long way off," the men answered. "The King and his advisers have troubles of their own. They forget us and our needs."

But finally, after long years, England did send enough ships and men and officers to end the war. Abigail was almost sixteen when word came that the French had surrendered. The meetinghouse bells rang out the good news. Everybody flocked to church to join in prayers of thanksgiving.

Aunt Elizabeth sent for Mary and Abigail. "You must come to Boston," she wrote. "I can't bear for you to miss the excitement. They're having fireworks out over the bay at night. There's a huge bonfire on top of Beacon Hill that will burn for days and days. There will be dances and teas and a grand ball."

"I wish we could go," said Mary.

"Indeed, you must go," said Grandmother. "You must have the right kind of clothes, too.

You'll be invited everywhere." She went to the attic at Mount Wollaston, and opened trunks and pulled out lovely silk and satin gowns that had been stored away during the war. She sent for dressmakers. They sewed all day and night to make the dresses over to fit the girls.

Abigail kept saying to herself, "I mustn't let myself count on this visit too much. It would be just my luck to get sick and not be able to go." But when the time came to leave, she was well and as gay and stylish as any young lady in the town. She went to all the parties in Boston and had a wonderful time. She wrote Father and Mother about everything she saw and heard.

"I'm glad now that you told me to let Abigail write letters," Mother said. "Reading her letters is almost the same as being in Boston. It's even better, for she sees more than I would."

"She's exactly where she belongs," said Father, "right in the center of things."

"It's never going to be the same around here again, though," said Phoebe. "Some young man's going to see our Nabby at those balls. He'll take her away from us."

Phoebe was right. Abigail was one of the most popular young ladies in Boston. She was invited everywhere. "She's so graceful," older people said, "and has beautiful manners."

"She's so pretty and bright and gay, no party is quite complete without her," her young friends said. "She's as kind as she is clever, too."

"There's no one like her," thought one young man in particular, and sought her out above all others. This was John Adams.

Everyone knew John. The Smiths knew him quite well, because he had been one of Father's students. Most people approved of him.

"He's one of the smartest young lawyers in the colony," Father said. He was pleased when John asked permission to court Abigail.

Mother wasn't. "He may be smart," she said, "but I think Nabby could do better. I'd rather she didn't marry a lawyer. Lawyers don't have the standing that ministers or doctors or even merchants have."

"John has," said Father. "The older men already look up to him and listen to what he has to say. He'll go far."

Grandfather Quincy agreed, but Mother remarked that John had a quick temper.

Abigail thought John was wonderful but she was prejudiced.

Abigail's Education

ALTHOUGH THE REVEREND SMITH was equally fond of all his children, he knew that Abigail understood his ways of thinking better than her sisters or her brother did. Beginning with that cold November day when he had baptized his tiny, frail daughter because he hardly expected her to live through the night, he had watched with delight the development of her keen mind.

Since she had not been strong enough to go to school, her father had been her tutor. He had encouraged her interest in reading books and in writing letters. He had taught her many things that most girls of her time knew nothing about.

He had never been able to arouse in Mary and William the wide interests and enthusiasms that Abigail had shown at such an early age. William was less concerned about politics than many of the other young men in Weymouth. Mary was quite willing to leave the affairs of the colonies to the men, and little Elizabeth seemed to be like her. Abigail, however, was vitally interested in whatever was happening in the colonies, and she had read most of the books in her father's and her grandfather's libraries.

Mount Wollaston, where Grandfather and Grandmother Quincy lived, was one of the finest farms in the neighborhood. The house was large and impressive, and the grounds sloped down to the sea. There were fields of fat cattle and fields of grain. There were a great many people to do the work, both inside the house and on the land. Thus there was time to give fine dinners, enjoy discussions, read, dream, and think.

Abigail, a favorite of her Grandmother Quincy, had frequently gone to Mount Wollaston for long visits. While she was there her grandmother had taken special pains to cultivate charm, courtesy, and grace in the little girl. She had dreamed of someday seeing this delicate, lovely child the mistress of an estate like Mount Wollaston, and she had prepared her granddaughter for it.

Grandmother had looked over the crop of boys who lived in the vicinity of Braintree, the town where Mount Wollaston was located. Several of them were industrious young men, sons of people she frequently entertained. They would eventually inherit wealth.

Abigail, grandmother hoped, would be the wife of one of these young men and live in a large, well-run home, with polished furniture, shining pewter and silver, fine linens, and thick rugs. She would manage such a home well.

Abigail liked to help Grandmother Quincy entertain the important people that Grandfather Quincy was always bringing home. Grandfather had been a member of the Massachusetts House of Representatives for many years. He had several other important offices, too, and Abigail liked to listen to Grandfather and his guests talk about the affairs of the colonies.

One of the most exciting things Grandfather did was to take charge of the affairs of the Ponkapoag Indians. These Indians walked the twelve miles from their reservation to Mount Wollaston whenever they needed help. They camped on the land, fished from the shore, and ate large amounts of food.

Grandmother and some of the people who worked on the farm did not like to have them come, for they helped themselves to wood, trapped animals, and ruined fences. Grandfather did not seem to mind.

Aunt Elizabeth and Uncle Isaac in Boston had other plans for Abigail. When the child did not go to Mount Wollaston to get better after one of her frequent illnesses, she went for long visits to Boston. She was a welcome visitor there, too. Aunt Elizabeth said that Abigail was a little lady and a very bright child.

As Abigail grew older Aunt Elizabeth saw to it that her niece met the sons of ship owners and other important people in Boston. Abigail liked the dances, teas, and other entertainments which were planned for the young people, but she was even more interested in all the things that were happening in Boston. It was fun to live in the largest city in the colonies.

Aunt Elizabeth smiled indulgently when Abigail got excited over the way the English governed the colonies. She hoped her niece would marry a Boston ship owner and forget problems that only men knew anything about.

All these people who loved Abigail had a part in making her an outstanding young woman. Her father had taught her to love reading and had encouraged her to read books that few women read in those days. In fact, a little reading and arithmetic was usually all the education considered necessary for a woman.

Her father and grandfather had provided fine libraries from which she could choose her books. Both of them had provided stimulating company —people who were interested in freedom, the governors appointed by the crown, the rights of Englishmen, and other matters that were of concern to the colonists. If she had not had the opportunity to listen to such discussions, she would have known very little about the exciting events that were happening.

Her mother and grandmother had taught her how to sew, bake, and perform expertly the many arts and skills needed to run a colonial home.

Grandmother Quincy and Aunt Elizabeth had taught her manners and charm. She knew what to say and how to act in the best company.

By the time Abigail was seventeen, she was one of the best-informed and best-educated girls in the colonies. She was also pretty, lively, and gay. Her friends considered her the wittiest person in their group.

Abigail Smith
and John Adams

THE SMITH family didn't think much about it at first when young John Adams came to the parsonage rather often with Richard Cranch. Richard, who was courting Mary, was a frequent visitor, and John often accompanied him to the house. By the time Mary was married, John Adams had asked permission to court eighteen-year-old Abigail.

The family—this included grandparents, cousins, aunts, and uncles—had expected the witty, delicate Abigail to make a brilliant marriage. Yet it was Mary who was marrying an outstanding man. Richard was already a partner in the glassworks at Braintree.

To be sure the Adamses were hard-working, honest farmers. But John's father had never been anything more important than a deacon and a militia officer. Grandfather Quincy had been a member of the Massachusetts House of Representatives for years. Now he was Speaker of the House. He was always elected moderator of the town meeting at Braintree, too, and he usually had two or three other offices.

A parson in any New England town was an important person who was treated with respect, and the Reverend William Smith was no exception. Many of Abigail's other relatives, such as Uncle Isaac in Boston, were outstanding people.

"Young John Adams is beginning to be quite well known in Boston," said the parson.

"I've heard that he's made a great many enemies because he has such a sharp tongue," Mrs. Smith said. "He'll never get very far because he can't get along with people."

"He always speaks his mind, and that's no way to get ahead," said a cousin.

"His father offered him the choice of having a share of the family farm or going to college," said another cousin. "He went to college, but he'd have been wiser to stay on the farm. Nobody can succeed as a lawyer in these troubled times. Even the young men with good family connections don't stand a chance."

"He was one of the best students in his class at Harvard," said the Reverend Smith. "Twenty-four young men graduated, too."

"At least John's a hard worker," Grandfather Quincy said. "He studied law while he was teaching school at Worcester. He must have spent all his spare time studying. You know he qualified for the bar with Sam Quincy."

"Wasn't John Adams interested in Sam's sister Hannah a year or two ago?" asked the cousin. "I used to meet him there rather often."

"He came to the house quite often for tea or for the evening," said Grandmother Quincy. "I think Hannah and her cousin Esther taught him a little bit about manners. He's not quite so shy and awkward as he used to be."

"He may be awkward, but he certainly isn't at all shy," said the cousin. "Sam brought him to a party after the two of them had spent the day in court not long ago. I was a guest, and so were some of the most important ladies and gentlemen in Boston. He has some unusual ideas, and he doesn't hesitate to express them. People listen to what he says, too."

"Well, he's an ambitious young man," said the Reverend Smith. "You know his father left him that house next to the Adams homestead and over nine acres of land. John's been working like a beaver to get the house and grounds in shape for Abigail. He's been busy in court, too, and he's kept on with his studies."

"I thought Nabby would marry a handsome man," said little Elizabeth. "Nabby is so pretty, and John is so short and plump."

Thus the Smiths and the Quincys discussed Abigail's suitor. They agreed that Abigail was marrying beneath her.

None of them suspected that John Adams would be the first Vice President and the second President of the new country that had not yet come into being. They did not know that he would be one of the most influential men of his age.

They had no idea that John would make Abigail the First Lady of the Land. How amazed they would have been to know that she would be the wife of one President of the United States and the mother of another!

Abigail's Marriage

JOHN COURTED Abigail for three years. During that time he was a very busy lawyer, and he was prospering. Sometimes he could come to see her frequently, for they lived only four miles apart. At other times he was so busy, or his work took him so far away that he was unable to come to Weymouth. Then the lovers wrote long letters to each other.

In the fall of 1764, when Abigail was twenty and John was twenty-seven, Parson Smith married them in the little church at Weymouth. It was a quiet wedding, and after the ceremony they went to live in John's house at Braintree.

A few days before, the Adams cart had come to carry the things Abigail wished to take from her father's house to her new home.

John was proud of Abigail's wit and beauty, and he thought she was the best-educated woman he had ever met. He liked to tell her about what he was doing and how he felt about the things that were happening in the colonies. Through John, Abigail felt as if she was a part of the exciting events of the times.

The small house to which John brought his bride was not at all like the great Quincy homestead or the fine town house of Uncle Isaac. But he had made the little home as snug and comfortable as possible, and Abigail loved it.

They entered the house hand in hand. In later years she would live with John in Boston, London, New York, Philadelphia, and Washington, but she would always think of Braintree as her home and long to be there.

John and Abigail were very happy for the next few years. John prospered, and he was beginning to be known, not only in Massachusetts but in the rest of the colonies, as an influential leader. He had had to spend a great deal of time in Boston, and his family had moved there to be with him for a while.

For some time the colonists had been demanding more freedom to govern themselves than the British were willing to give them. There were frequent clashes between the British soldiers and the colonists in Boston. John arranged for Abigail and their children to return to the little house in Braintree. He thought his family would be safe there.

John Adams was taking a more and more active part in the cause of liberty for the colonists. He knew that he might be imprisoned or killed by the British. He was worried about Abigail and their children.

"You must think of your duty before you think of us," Abigail told him. "You can do certain things for the colonies that no one else can."

"I wish I could stay home and protect you and our children," said John.

"Don't be afraid for us," Abigail said. "Liberty is more important than peace. I want you to do your part in this struggle."

One day John came home and told Abigail, "There is going to be a Continental Congress in Philadelphia in September, and I have been appointed one of the delegates. We will have to decide how the colonies can get their rights."

More than fifty of the wisest men in the colonies came to the First Continental Congress at Philadelphia. Among them were Colonel George Washington and Mr. Patrick Henry.

Before long John Adams had to return to Philadelphia to go to the Second Continental Congress.

One hot morning in June Abigail was awakened about three o'clock by some unusual sound. At first she thought she heard thunder, but the sky was clear. Suddenly she realized she was hearing guns. Abigail ran to the top of the highest hill in the vicinity with her spy glass. Her eight-year-old son, John Quincy, went too.

"Does that fire and smoke come from cannons, Mother?" asked John Quincy. "Are we looking at a real battle?"

"Yes, Johnny," his mother replied. "This very battle may decide the future of the colonies."

When they returned to the house little Abigail, Johnny's older sister, looking frightened herself, was trying to quiet the fears of her young brothers, Charles and baby Tommy.

Soon Abigail and John Quincy went back to watch the battle. John Quincy never forgot that June day in 1775. He remembered the Battle of Bunker Hill as long as he lived.

"It has not ceased yet," Abigail wrote to John that night. "...a dreadful battle must ensue... How many have fallen we know not. The constant roar of the cannon is so distressing that we cannot eat, drink or sleep."

When the battle was over they heard that the Americans, after repulsing the British twice, had run out of ammunition and had had to flee. However, the British had lost about 1,000 soldiers. The Americans had 145 soldiers killed, and about 300 wounded and prisoners.

Busy as they were, John and Abigail wrote letters to each other almost every day and sent them by messenger on the 400 mile journey. John bought a notebook in Philadelphia to keep copies of his letters.

He told her that he had nominated George Washington to be commander in chief of the Continental army and that Colonel Washington had been appointed.

He wrote her that he was on a committee with Thomas Jefferson and Benjamin Franklin to draft a Declaration of Independence. Abigail was very proud to know that John had such an important part in forming the new nation.

Abigail had to write that their three-year-old son Tommy was very ill. She kept his cradle beside her as she wrote the letter.

John Adams was sent as ambassador to France, and he took John Quincy with him. Abigail remained at home to manage the farm, care for her other children, and encourage and help her relatives and neighbors.

After that he was sent to Great Britain to arrange a treaty with Great Britain. This was an even greater honor. He sailed, taking both John Quincy and Charles with him this time.

After he made a treaty with Great Britain, he sent for Abigail to join him in England. She crossed the ocean to be with him. She was the first woman from the United States to meet the Queen of England.

The Queen didn't want to meet her. She didn't want to meet anyone from America. "Who is this Mrs. Adams?" she asked her ladies in waiting.

"She's the daughter of a village preacher somewhere near Boston," said one of the ladies. "She won't know what to do at court."

"I'd like to know why I, the Queen, should meet a country bumpkin as an equal," said the Queen haughtily. She sulked and kept Abigail standing in the anteroom for four hours waiting for her. While she waited, Abigail asked herself almost the same question.

"After all," she thought, "who am I, Abigail Smith Adams, that I should meet a queen?"

She had plenty of time to think about it. She thought back over the years of the Revolution. She remembered the women who had run the farms while the men were at war. She remembered how they had kept at their tasks, in spite of hardships, day after day without complaining.

"They were wonderful, those American women," she said to herself, "and I'm here to represent them. I'm not here as Nabby Adams."

Abigail held her head high when she met the Queen. "The American lady is more like a Queen than the Queen herself," the ladies said.

While John and Abigail were in England they heard that the new United States did not have enough money to carry on. It was Abigail who suggested that John go to Holland to get a loan to help their new country meet its debts. They were able to return to the United States soon after he had completed this mission.

"Home again at last," said Abigail when she and John returned to America. "Now surely we can go back to Braintree."

But the young country had need of John Adam's services for many years more. There were many honors yet to come for John and Abigail. It was a long time before they could settle down in their own home.

Wife of the Vice President

THE WHOLE COUNTRY wanted Washington to be the first President of the United States. Another man who could be trusted was needed for Vice President. John Adams was chosen for the first Vice President of the United States.

Abigail had to get the farm in order, see to the business affairs, and care for her children. The seat of the government was in New York at that time, and John had to go on the journey by himself. Abigail would follow as soon as she could. She wished she could go with him. She wanted to be there for the ceremonies, which were held March 4, 1789.

She heard proudly of the crowds that greeted him all along the way. The people appreciated all that John Adams had done for his country.

Abigail traveled to New York by boat. This boat stopped at several ports along the way to take on passengers. Mrs. Adams was honored as much as her husband. Important people came to call on her and tell her how glad they were to have John Adams for Vice President.

John was presiding in the Senate and could not meet her when she reached New York. The captain of the boat took her to the beautiful house that John had found for her.

In a few days Abigail went to call on Mrs. Washington and enjoyed her visit very much.

"She is more dignified than the Queen of England," Abigail said.

Martha Washington and Abigail Adams soon were good friends. Mrs. Washington returned Abigail's call as soon as she could.

Philadelphia had been made the capital of the United States in 1790. John and Abigail found a large brick house with large grounds to live in. The grounds were very bare, however, for the British had used all the trees and bushes for firewood during the war. A shepherd brought his sheep every day to eat grass on the grounds. The children liked the sheep.

Abigail was not very well in Philadelphia, and John insisted on her returning to Braintree until she got over her illness. He came to stay with her on the farm in the summer. Then there was an epidemic of yellow fever in Philadelphia and he was afraid to have her return.

John was not the only one who missed Abigail in Philadelphia. Mrs. Washington wished she would come back, and many of the senators said the dinners and other state occasions were dull without her. Many people agreed that she had been the wittiest lady in Philadelphia.

When Abigail returned to their farm she soon felt better. She began to plan for the time when John would finish his term as Vice President and return to live there with her.

By this time the part of Braintree where her Grandfather Quincy's farm had been and most of the rest of the district had been renamed Quincy in honor of her grandfather.

The First Lady

AFTER GEORGE WASHINGTON had been President for eight years, John Adams was elected the second President of the United States. Abigail was now the First Lady of the Land.

While John was President, Congress made Washington, D. C., the capital and built a house for the President's family. Abigail was the first woman to live in the White House.

She set out for the new capital with high spirits. The journey to the new city was hard. The roads were little more than trails through the dense forest. Abigail cheered herself along the way by picturing the beautiful new home.

189

After days of travel, during which the driver lost his way, the horses came to a stop at the end of the road. They were in a swamp. There were only trees around them.

"The capital is a little farther on," said the driver. "This is as far as the coach can go."

Abigail walked through the mud with a sinking heart. Then she saw the beautiful house ahead of her. When she got to the door, however, no one met her or answered her knock. The house was empty, damp, and cold.

She discovered that the servants had left because there was no place for them to stay in the wilderness. The city wasn't built yet.

Abigail knew that invitations had already been sent out for a reception which was to be held in a month. Ambassadors from foreign courts were invited. She was tired and ill, but when something had to be done, she did it. When the day for the reception came, she was ready.

The guests, after floundering through mud to the unfinished mansion, were received graciously by the President and his Lady in the beautiful oval room. It looked dignified and cheerful with hundreds of candles and great roaring fires.

Although Abigail was ill during most of her life she was a great help to her husband during all the fifty-four years of their marriage. For long periods John Adams was away from home working for his country. During those times Abigail took care of their children, managed the farm, and helped her neighbors.

She is the only woman to be the wife of one of our presidents and the mother of another. John Quincy Adams, who watched the Battle of Bunker Hill with his mother, became the sixth President of the United States.

When we read letters she wrote to members of her family and to friends, we can perceive her character, patriotism, and devotion to duty.